J. M. Coetzee
Age of Iron

J. M. COETZEE is one of South Africa's most distin-
guished novelists, the author of *Dusklands, In the Heart of
the Country, Waiting for the Barbarians,* the Booker Prize-
winning *Life & Times of Michael K,* and *Foe.* He is a profes-
sor of general literature at the University of Cape Town.

VINTAGE

INTERNATIONAL

Age of Iron

Vintage International • Vintage Books

A Division of Random House, Inc. • New York

Age of Iron

J. M. Coetzee

FIRST VINTAGE INTERNATIONAL EDITION, JUNE 1992

Copyright © 1990 by J.M. Coetzee

Library of Congress Cataloging-in-Publication Data
Coetzee, J.M., 1940–
Age of iron / J.M. Coetzee. —1st Vintage International ed.
p. cm.
ISBN 0-679-73292-6 (pbk.)
I. Title.
[PR9369.3.C58A7 1992]
823—dc20   91-50096
CIP

Book design by Debbie Glasserman

Author photo © Jerry Bauer

Manufactured in the United States of America
10 9 8 7 6 5 4 3 2 1

Age of Iron

one

There is an alley down the side of the garage, you may remember it, you and your friends would sometimes play there. Now it is a dead place, waste, without use, where windblown leaves pile up and rot.

Yesterday, at the end of this alley, I came upon a house of carton boxes and plastic sheeting and a man curled up inside, a man I recognized from the streets: tall, thin, with a weathered skin and long, carious fangs, wearing a baggy gray suit and a hat with a sagging brim. He had the hat on now, sleeping with the brim folded under his ear. A derelict, one of the derelicts who hang around the parking lots on Mill Street, cadging money from shoppers, drinking under the overpass, eating out of refuse cans. One of the homeless for whom August, month of rains, is the worst month. Asleep in his box, his legs stretched out like a marionette's, his jaw agape. An unsavory smell about him: urine, sweet wine, moldy clothing, and something else too. Unclean.

For a while I stood staring down on him, staring and smelling. A visitor, visiting himself on me on this of all days.

This was the day when I had the news from Dr. Syfret. The news was not good, but it was mine, for me, mine only, not to be refused. It was for me to take in my arms and fold to my chest and take home, without headshaking, without tears. "Thank you, doctor," I said. "Thank you for being frank." "We will do everything we can," he said, "we will tackle this together." But already, behind the comradely front, I could see he was withdrawing. *Sauve qui peut.* His allegiance to the living, not the dying.

The trembling began only when I got out of the car. By the time I had closed the garage door I was shaking all over: to still it I had to clench my teeth, grip my handbag. It was then that I saw the boxes, saw him.

"What are you doing here?" I demanded, hearing the irritation in my voice, not checking it. "You can't stay, you must go."

He did not stir, lying in his shelter, looking up, inspecting the winter stockings, the blue coat, the skirt with whose hang there has always been something wrong, the gray hair cut by a strip of scalp, old woman's scalp, pink, babyish.

Then he drew in his legs and leisurely got up. Without a word he turned his back on me, shook out the black plastic,

4 I

folded it in half, in quarters, in eighths. He produced a bag (AIR CANADA, it said) and zipped it shut, I stood aside. Leaving behind the boxes, an empty bottle, and a smell of urine, he passed me. His trousers sagged; he hitched them up. I waited to be sure he had gone, and heard him stow the plastic in the hedge from the other side.

Two things, then, in the space of an hour: the news, long dreaded, and this reconnaissance, this other annunciation. The first of the carrion birds, prompt, unerring. How long can I fend them off? The scavengers of Cape Town, whose number never dwindles. Who go bare and feel no cold. Who sleep outdoors and do not sicken. Who starve and do not waste. Warmed from within by alcohol. The contagions and infections in their blood consumed in liquid flame. Cleaners-up after the feast. Flies, dry-winged, glazen-eyed, pitiless. My heirs.

With what slow steps did I enter this empty house, from which every echo has faded, where the very tread of footsole on board is flat and dull! How I longed for you to be here, to hold me, comfort me! I begin to understand the true meaning of the embrace. We embrace to be embraced. We embrace our children to be folded in the arms of the future, to pass ourselves on beyond death, to be transported. That is how it was when I embraced you, always. We bear children in order to be mothered by them. Home truths, a mother's truth: from now to the end that is all you will hear from me. So: how I longed for you! How I longed to be able to go upstairs to you, to sit on your bed, run my fingers through your hair, whisper in your ear as I did on school mornings, "Time to get up!" And then, when you turned over, your body blood-warm, your breath milky, to take you in my arms in what we called "giving Mommy a big hug," the secret meaning of which, the meaning never spoken, was that Mommy should not be sad, for she would not die but live on in you.

To live! You are my life; I love you as I love life itself. In the mornings I come out of the house and wet my finger and hold it up to the wind. When the chill is from the northwest, from your quarter, I stand a long time sniffing, concentrating my attention in the hope that across ten thousand miles of land and sea some breath will reach me of the milkiness you still carry with you behind your ears, in the fold of your neck.

The first task laid on me, from today: to resist the craving to share my death. Loving you, loving life, to forgive the living and take my leave without bitterness. To embrace death as my own, mine alone.

To whom this writing then? The answer: to you but not to you; to me; to you in me.

All afternoon I tried to keep myself busy, cleaning out drawers, sorting and discarding papers. At dusk I came out again. Behind the garage the shelter was set up as before, with the black plastic neatly spanned over it. Inside lay the man, his legs curled up, and a dog beside him that cocked its ears and wagged its tail. A collie, young, little more than a pup, black, with white points.

"No fires," I said. "Do you understand? I want no fires, I want no mess."

He sat up, rubbing his bare ankles, staring around as if not knowing where he was. A horsy, weather-beaten face with the puffiness around the eyes of an alcoholic. Strange green eyes: unhealthy.

"Do you want something to eat?" I said.

He followed me to the kitchen, the dog at his heels, and waited while I cut him a sandwich. He took a bite but then seemed to forget to chew, standing against the doorjamb with his mouth full, the light shining into his vacant green eyes, while the dog whined softly. "I have to clean up," I said impatiently, and made to close the door on him. He went off without a murmur; but before he turned the corner I was sure I saw him toss the sandwich away, and the dog dive after it.

There were not so many of these homeless people in your time. But now they are part of life here. Do they frighten me? On the whole, no. A little begging, a little thieving; dirt, noise, drunkenness; no worse. It is the roaming gangs I fear, the sullen-mouthed boys, rapacious as sharks, on whom the first shade of the prison house is already beginning to close. Children scorning childhood, the time of wonder, the growing time of the soul. Their souls, their organs of wonder, stunted, petrified. And on the other side of the great divide their white cousins soul-stunted too, spinning themselves tighter and tighter into their sleepy cocoons. Swimming lessons, riding lessons, ballet lessons; cricket on the lawn; lives passed within walled gardens guarded by bulldogs; children of paradise, blond, innocent, shining with angelic light, soft as *putti*. Their residence the limbo of the unborn, their innocence the innocence of bee grubs, plump and white, drenched in honey, absorbing sweetness through their soft skins. Slumbrous their souls, bliss-filled, abstracted.

Why do I give this man food? For the same reason I would feed his dog (stolen, I am sure) if it came begging. For the same reason I gave you my breast. To be full enough to give and to give from one's fullness: what deeper urge is there? Out of their withered bodies even the old try to squeeze one last drop. A stubborn will to give, to nourish. Shrewd was death's aim when he chose my breast for his first shaft.

This morning, bringing him coffee, I found him urinating into the drain, which he did without any appearance of shame.

"Do you want a job of work?" I said. "There are plenty of jobs I can give you."

He said nothing, but drank the coffee, holding the mug in both hands.

"You are wasting your life," I said. "You are not a child anymore. How can you live like this? How can you lie around and do nothing all day? I don't understand it."

It is true: I do not understand it. Something in me revolts at the lassitude, the letting go, the welcoming of dissolution.

He did something that shocked me. With a straight look, the first direct look he has given me, he spat a gob of spit, thick, yellow, streaked with brown from the coffee, onto the concrete beside my foot. Then he thrust the mug at me and sauntered off.

The thing itself, I thought, shaken: the thing itself brought out between us. Spat not upon me but before me, where I could see it, inspect it, think about it. His word, his kind of word, from his own mouth, warm at the instant when it left him. A word, undeniable, from a language before language. First the look and then the spitting. What kind of look? A look without respect, from a man to a woman old enough to be his mother. Here: take your coffee.

He did not sleep in the alley last night. The boxes are gone too. But, poking around, I came upon the Air Canada bag in the woodshed, and a place that he must have scratched for himself amid the jumble of lumber and faggots. So I know he means to come back.

Six pages already, and all about a man you have never met and never will. Why do I write about him? Because he is and is not I. Because in the look he gives me I see myself in a way that can be written. Otherwise what would this writing be but a kind of moaning, now high, now low? When I write about him I write about myself. When I write about his dog I write about myself; when I write about the house I write about myself. Man, house, dog: no matter what the word, through it I stretch out a hand to you. In another world I would not need words. I would appear on your doorstep. "I have come for a visit," I would say, and that would be the end of words: I would embrace you and be embraced. But in this world, in this time, I must reach out to you in words. So day by day I render myself into words and pack the words into the page like sweets: like sweets for my daughter, for her birthday, for the day of her birth. Words out of my body, drops of myself, for her to unpack in her own time, to take in, to suck, to absorb. As they say on the bottle: old-fashioned drops, drops fashioned by the old, fashioned and packed with love, the love we have no alternative but to feel toward those to whom we give ourselves to devour or discard.

Though it rained steadily all afternoon, it was not till dark that I heard the creak of the gate and, a minute later, the click of the dog's claws on the veranda.

I was watching television. One of the tribe of *ministers* and *onderministers* was making an announcement to the nation. I was standing, as I always do when they speak, as a way of keeping what I can of my self-respect (who would choose to face a firing squad sitting down?). *Ons buig nie voor dreigemente nie,* he was saying: we do not bow to threats: one of those speeches.

The curtains behind me were open. At a certain moment I became aware of him, the man whose name I do not know, watching over my shoulder through the glass. So I turned up the sound, enough for, if not the words, then the cadences to reach him, the slow, truculent Afrikaans rhythms with their deadening closes, like a hammer beating a post into the ground. Together, blow after blow, we listened. The disgrace of the life one lives under them: to open a newspaper, to switch on the television, like kneeling and being urinated on. Under them: under their meaty bellies, their full bladders. "Your days are numbered," I used to whisper once upon a time, to them who will now outlast me.

I was on my way out to the shops, in the act of opening the garage door, when I had a sudden attack. An attack: it was just that: the pain hurling itself upon me like a dog, sinking its teeth into my back. I cried out, unable to stir. Then he, this man, appeared from somewhere and helped me into the house.

I lay down on the sofa, on my left side, in the only comfortable posture left to me. He waited. "Sit down." I said. He sat. The pain began to subside. "I have cancer," I said. "It has made its way into the bone. That is what hurts."

I was not at all sure he understood.

A long silence. Then: "This is a big house," he said. "You could turn it into a boarding house."

I made a tired gesture.

"You could let rooms to students," he went on relentlessly.

I yawned, and, feeling my teeth sag, covered my mouth. Once upon a time I would have blushed. But no longer.

"I have a woman who helps with the housework," I said. "She is away till the end of the month, visiting her people. Do you have people?"

A curious expression: to have people. Do I have people? Are you my people? I think not. Perhaps only Florence qualifies to have people.

He made no reply. There is an air of childlessness about him. Of having no children in the world but also of having no childhood in his past. His face all bone and weathered skin. As one cannot imagine a snake's head that does not look old, so one cannot see behind his face the face of a child. Green eyes, animal eyes: can one picture an infant with eyes like that?

"My husband and I parted a long time ago," I said. "He is dead now. I have a daughter in America. She left in 1976 and hasn't come back. She is married to an American. They have two children of their own."

A daughter. Flesh of my flesh. You.

He took out a packet of cigarettes. "Don't smoke in the house, please," I said.

"What is your disability?" I said. "You say you get a disability pension."

He held out his right hand. Thumb and forefinger stood out; the other three fingers curled into the palm. "I can't move them," he said.

We gazed at his hand, at the three crooked fingers with their dirty nails. Not what I would call a work-callused hand.

"Was it an accident?"

He nodded; the kind of nod that committed him to nothing. "I'll pay you to cut the lawn," I said.

For an hour, using the hedge clippers, he hacked listlessly at the grass, knee-high by now in places. In the end he had cleared a patch a few yards square. Then he quit. "It's not my kind of work," he said. I paid him for the hour. As he left he bumped against the cat tray, spilling litter all over the veranda.

All in all, more trouble than he is worth. But I did not choose him. He chose me. Or perhaps he merely chose the one house without a dog. A house of cats.

The cats are unsettled by these newcomers. When they show their noses outside the dog makes playful dashes at them, so they skulk indoors, peevish. Today they would not eat. Thinking they spurned the food because it had been in the refrigerator, I stirred a little hot water into the smelly mess (what is it? seal flesh? whale flesh?). Still they disdained it, circling the dish, flicking the tips of their tails. "Eat!" I said, pushing the dish at them. The big one lifted a finicky paw to avoid being touched. At which I lost control. "Go to hell, then!" I screamed, and flung the fork wildly in their direction—"I am sick to death of feeding you!" In my voice there was a new, mad edge; and, hearing it, I exulted. Enough of being nice to people, enough of being nice to cats! "Go to hell!" I screamed again, at the top of my voice. Their claws scrabbled on the linoleum as they fled.

Who cares? When I am in a mood like this I am capable of putting a hand on the breadboard and chopping it off without a second thought. What do I care for this body that has betrayed me? I look at my hand and see only a tool, a hook, a thing for gripping other things. And these legs, these clumsy, ugly stilts: why should I have to carry them with me everywhere? Why should I take them to bed with me night after night and pack them in under the sheets, and pack the arms in too, higher up near the face, and lie there sleepless amid the clutter? The abdomen too, with its dead gurglings, and the heart beating, beating: why? What have they to do with me?

We sicken before we die so that we will be weaned from our body. The milk that nourished us grows thin and sour; turning away from the breast, we begin to be restless for a separate life. Yet this first life, this life on earth, on the body of earth—will there, can there ever be a better? Despite all the glooms and despairs and rages, I have not let go of my love of it.

In pain, I took two of Dr. Syfret's pills and lay down on the sofa. Hours later I woke befuddled and cold, fumbled my way upstairs, got into bed without undressing.

In the middle of the night I became aware of a presence in the room that could only have been his. A presence or a smell. It was there, then it went away.

From the landing came a creak. Now he is entering the study, I thought; now he is switching on the light. I tried to recall whether, among the papers on the desk, any were private, but there was too much confusion in my head. Now he sees the books, shelf upon shelf, I thought, trying to bring back order, and the piles of old journals. Now he looks at the pictures on the wall: Sophie Schliemann decked out in Agamemnon's treasure hoard; the robed Demeter from the British Museum. Now, quietly, he slides out the drawers of the desk. The top drawer, full of letters, accounts, torn-off stamps, photographs, does not interest him. But in the bottom drawer there is a cigar box full of coins: pennies, drachmas, centimes, schillings. The hand with the curled fingers dips into it, takes out two five-peseta pieces big enough to pass for rands, pockets them.

Not an angel, certainly. An insect, rather, emerging from behind the baseboards when the house is in darkness to forage for crumbs.

I heard him at the far end of the landing, trying the two locked doors. Only rubbish, I wanted to whisper to him— rubbish and dead memories; but the fog in my head closed in again.

Spent the day in bed. No energy, no appetite. Read Tolstoy— not the famous cancer story, which I know all too well, but the story of the angel who takes up residence with the shoe-maker. What chance is there, if I take a walk down to Mill Street, of finding my own angel to bring home and succor? None, I think. Perhaps in the countryside there are still one or two sitting against milestones in the heat of the sun, dozing, waiting for what chance will bring. Perhaps in the squatter camps. But not in Mill Street, not in the suburbs. The suburbs, deserted by the angels. When a ragged stranger comes knock-ing at the door he is never anything but a derelict, an alcoholic, a lost soul. Yet how, in our hearts, we long for these sedate homes of ours to tremble, as in the story, with angelic chant-ing!

This house is tired of waiting for the day, tired of holding itself together. The floorboards have lost their spring. The insulation of the wiring is dry, friable, the pipes clogged with grit. The gutters sag where screws have rusted away or pulled loose from the rotten wood. The roof tiles are heavy with moss. A house built solidly but without love, cold, inert now, ready to die. Whose walls the sun, even the African sun, has never succeeded in warming, as though the very bricks, made by the hands of convicts, radiate an intractable sullenness.

Last summer, when the workmen were re-laying the drains, I watched them dig out the old pipes. Two meters down into the earth they went, bringing up moldering brick, rusty iron, even a solitary horseshoe. But no bones. A site without a human past; to spirits, as to angels, of no interest.

This letter is not a baring of my heart. It is a baring of something, but not of my heart.

Since the car would not start this morning, I had to ask him, this man, this lodger, to push. He pushed me down the drive-way. "Now!" he shouted, slapping the roof. The engine caught. I swung into the road, drove a few yards, then, on an impulse, stopped. "I have to go to Fish Hoek," I called from a cloud of smoke. "Do you want to come along?"

So we set off, the dog on the back seat, in the green Hillman of your childhood. For a long while no word passed between us. Past the hospital, past the University, past Bishopscourt we drove, the dog leaning over my shoulder to feel the wind on its face. Up Wynberg Hill we toiled. On the long downhill swoop on the other side I switched off the engine and coasted. Faster and faster we went, till the wheel shuddered in my hands and the dog whined with excitement. I was smiling, I believe; my eyes may even have been shut.

At the foot of the hill, as we began to slow down, I cast him a glance. He sat relaxed, imperturbable. Good man! I thought.

"When I was a child," I said, "I used to do downhills on a bicycle with no brakes to speak of. It belonged to my elder brother. He would dare me. I was completely without fear. Children cannot conceive of what it is to die. It never crosses their minds that they may not be immortal.

"I would ride my brother's bicycle down hills even steeper than this one. The faster I went, the more alive I would feel. I would quiver with life as if I were about to burst through my skin. As a butterfly must feel when it is being born, or bearing itself.

"In an old car like this you still have the freedom to coast. With a modern car, when you switch off the engine the steering wheel locks. I am sure you know that. But people sometimes make a mistake or forget, and then can't keep the car on the road. Sometimes they go over the side and into the sea."

Into the sea. Tussling with a locked wheel while you soar in a bubble of glass over the sun-glinting sea. Does it really happen? Do many do it? If I stood on Chapman's Peak on a Saturday afternoon, would I see them, men and women, thick in the air as midges taking off on their last flight?

"There is a story I want to tell you," I said. "When my mother was still a child, in the early years of the century, the family used to go to the seaside for Christmas. This was still in the age of ox wagons. They would travel by ox wagon all the way from Uniondale in the Eastern Cape to Plettenberg Bay at the mouth of the Piesangs River, a journey of a hundred miles taking I don't know how many days. Along the way they would camp at the roadside.

"One of their stopping places was at the top of a mountain pass. My grandparents would spend the nights in the wagon itself while my mother and the other children had their bed underneath it. So—here the story begins—my mother lay at the top of the pass in the stillness of the night, snug in her blankets with her brothers and sisters sleeping beside her, watching the stars through the spokes of the wheels. As she watched, it began to seem that the stars were moving: the stars were moving or else the wheels were moving, slowly, very slowly. She thought: What shall I do? What if the wagon is beginning to roll? Shall I call out a warning? What if I lie silent and the wagon gathers speed and rolls all the way down the mountainside with my parents inside? But what if I am imagining it all?

"Choking with fear, her heart pounding, she lay there watching the stars, watching them move, thinking, Shall I? Shall I? listening for the creak, the first creak. At last she fell asleep, and her sleep was full of dreams of death. But in the morning, when she reemerged, it was into light and peace. And the wagon reemerged with her, and her parents reemerged, and all was well, as it had been before."

It was time for him to say something now, about hills or cars or bicycles or about himself or his childhood. But he was stubbornly silent.

"She told no one what went on in the night," I resumed. "Perhaps she was waiting for me to come. I heard the story many times from her, in many forms. Always they were on their way to the Piesangs River. Such a lovely golden name!

I was sure it must be the most beautiful place on earth. Years after my mother's death I visited Plettenberg Bay and saw the Piesangs River for the first time. Not a river at all, just a trickle of water choked with reeds, and mosquitoes in the evenings, and a caravan park full of screaming children and fat barefoot men in shorts braaiing sausages over gas cookers. Not Paradise at all. Not a place one would mount a journey to year after year through valleys and over mountains."

Up Boyes Drive the car was laboring now, willing but old, like Rocinante. I gripped the wheel tighter, urging her on.

Above Muizenberg, overlooking the sweep of False Bay, I parked and switched off the engine. The dog began to whine. We let it out. It sniffed the curbstones, sniffed the bushes, relieved itself, while we watched in awkward silence.

He spoke. "You are pointing the wrong way," he said. "You should be pointing downhill."

I hid my chagrin. I have always wished to be thought a capable person. Now more than ever, with incapability looming.

"Are you from the Cape?" I said.

"Yes."

"And have you lived here all your life?"

He shifted restlessly. Two questions: one too many.

A breaker, perfectly straight, hundreds of yards long, rolled inshore, a single crouched figure on a surfboard gliding ahead of it. Across the bay the mountains of Hottentots Holland stood out clear and blue. Hunger, I thought: it is a hunger of the eyes that I feel, such hunger that I am loath even to blink. These seas, these mountains: I want to burn them upon my sight so deeply that, no matter where I go, they will always be before me. I am hungry with love of this world.

A flock of sparrows settled on the bushes around us, preened themselves, took off again. The surfer reached shore and began to trudge up the beach. Suddenly there were tears in my eyes. From not blinking, I told myself. But the truth was, I was crying. Hunched over the wheel, I abandoned myself, first to a quiet, decent sobbing, then to long wails without articulation, emptyings of the lungs, emptyings of the heart. "I am so sorry," I gasped; and then, when I was calmer: "I am sorry, I don't know what has come over me."

I should not have bothered to apologize. He gave no sign of having noticed anything.

I dried my eyes, blew my nose. "Shall we go?" I said.

He opened the door, gave a long whistle. The dog bounded in. An obedient dog, no doubt stolen from a good family.

The car was indeed pointing the wrong way.

"Start in reverse," he said.

I released the hand brake, rolled back down the hill a little way, let out the clutch. The car shuddered and stopped. "It has never started in reverse," I said.

"Swing over to the other side of the road," he directed, like a husband giving a driving lesson.

I let the car roll further downhill, then swung across the road. With blaring horn a great white Mercedes shot past on the inside. "I didn't see it!" I gasped.

"Go!" he shouted.

I stared in astonishment at this stranger shouting at me. "Go!" he shouted again, straight into my face.

The engine caught. I drove back in stiff silence. At the corner of Mill Street he asked to be let off.

The worst of the smell comes from his shoes and feet. He needs socks. He needs new shoes. He needs a bath. He needs a bath every day; he needs clean underwear; he needs a bed, he needs a roof over his head, he needs three meals a day, he needs money in the bank. Too much to give: too much for someone who longs, if the truth be told, to creep into her own mother's lap and be comforted.

Late in the afternoon he returned. Making an effort to forget what had passed, I took him around the garden, pointing out tasks that need to be done. "Pruning, for instance," I said. "Do you know how to prune?"

He shook his head. No, he didn't know how to prune. Or didn't want to.

In the bottom corner, the most heavily overgrown, thick creepers covered the old oak bench and the rabbit hutch. "This should all be cleared," I said.

He lifted one edge of the mat of creepers. On the floor of the hutch was a jumble of parched bones, including the perfect skeleton of a young rabbit, its neck arched back in a last contortion.

"Rabbits," I said. "They used to belong to my domestic's son. I let him keep them here as pets. Then there was some commotion or other in his life. He forgot about them and they starved to death. I was in hospital and didn't know about it. I was terribly upset when I came back and found out what agony had been going on unheeded at the bottom of the garden. Creatures that can't talk, that can't even cry."

Guavas were dropping, worm-riddled, making a malodorous pulpy carpet under the tree. "I wish the trees would stop bearing," I said. "But they never do."

The dog, following behind, sniffed perfunctorily at the hutch. The dead long dead, their smells all gone.

"Anyhow, do what you can to bring it back under control," I said. "So that it doesn't become a complete wilderness."

"Why?" he said.

"Because that is how I am," I said. "Because I don't mean to leave a mess behind."

He shrugged, smiling to himself.

"If you want to be paid you will have to earn it," I said. "I am not giving you money for nothing."

For the rest of the afternoon he worked, hacking away at the creepers and grass, pausing now and again to stare into the distance, pretending not to be aware that I was keeping an eye on him from upstairs. At five o'clock I paid him. "I know you are not a gardener," I said, "and I don't want to turn you into what you are not. But we can't proceed on a basis of charity."

Taking the notes, folding them, putting them in his pocket, looking off to one side so as not to look at me, he said softly, "Why?"

"Because you don't deserve it."

And he, smiling, keeping his smile to himself: "Deserve . . . Who deserves anything?"

Who deserves anything? In a quick fury I thrust the purse at him. "What do you believe in, then? Taking? Taking what you want? Go on: take!"

Calmly he took the purse, emptied it of thirty rand and some coins, and handed it back. Then off he went, the dog jauntily at his heels. In half an hour he was back; I heard the clink of bottles.

Somewhere he has found himself a mattress, one of those folding mattresses people take to the beach. In his little nest amid the dust and mess of the woodshed, with a candle at his head and the dog at his feet, he lay smoking.

"I want that money back," I said.

He reached into his pocket and held out some notes. I took them. Not all the money, but that did not matter.

"If you are in need, you can ask," I said. "I am not a stingy person. And be careful with that candle. I don't want a fire."

I turned and went. But in a minute was back.

"You told me," I said, "that I should turn this house into a boardinghouse for students. Well, there are better things I could do with it. I could turn it into a haven for beggars. I could run a soup kitchen and a dormitory. But I don't. Why not? Because the spirit of charity has perished in this country. Because those who accept charity despise it, while those who give give with a despairing heart. What is the point of charity when it does not go from heart to heart? What do you think charity is? Soup? Money? *Charity:* from the Latin word for the heart. It is as hard to receive as to give. It takes as much effort. I wish you would learn that. I wish you would learn something instead of just lying around."

A lie: charity, *caritas,* has nothing to do with the heart. But what does it matter if my sermons rest on false etymologies? He barely listens when I speak to him. Perhaps, despite those keen bird-eyes, he is more befuddled with drink than I know. Or perhaps, finally, he does not care. Care: the true root of charity. I look for him to care, and he does not. Because he is beyond caring. Beyond caring and beyond care.

Since life in this country is so much like life aboard a sinking ship, one of those old-time liners with a lugubrious, drunken captain and a surly crew and leaky lifeboats, I keep the short-wave radio at my bedside. Most of the time there is only talk to be heard; but if one persists into the unlikely hours of the night there are stations that relent and play music. Fading in, fading out, I heard last night—from where? Helsinki? the Cook Islands?—anthems of all the nations, celestial music, music that left us years ago and now comes back from the stars transfigured, gentle, as evidence that all that is given forth will at length return. A closed universe, curved like an egg, enclosing us.

There I lay in the dark, listening to the music of the stars and the crackling and humming that accompanied it like the dust of meteors, smiling, my heart filled with gratitude for this good news from afar. The one border they cannot close, I thought: the border upward, between the Republic of South Africa and the empire of the sky. Where I am due to travel. Where no passport is called for.

Still under the spell of the music (it was, I think, Stockhausen), I sat down at the piano this afternoon and played some of the old pieces: preludes from the Well-Tempered Clavier, Chopin preludes, Brahms waltzes, from Novello and Augener editions tattered, mottled, dry as dust. I played as badly as ever, misreading the same chords as half a century ago, repeating fingering mistakes grown by now into the bone, never to be corrected. (The bones prized above all by archaeologists, I remember, are those gnarled with disease or splintered by an arrowhead: bones marked with a history from a time before history.)

After I had tired of the sweetness of Brahms I closed my eyes and played chords, searching with my fingers for the one chord I would recognize, when I came upon it, as my chord, as what in the old days we used to call the lost chord, the heart's chord. (I speak of a time before your time, when, passing down the street on a hot Saturday afternoon, you might hear, faint but dogged from a front parlor, the maiden of the household groping among the keys for that yearned-for, elusive resonance. Days of charm and sorrow and mystery too! Days of innocence!)

"Jerusalem!" I sang softly, playing chords I last heard at my grandmother's knee. *"And was Jerusalem y-builded here?"*

Then at last I went back to Bach, and played clumsily, over and over again, the first fugue from Book One. The sound was muddy, the lines blurred, but every now and again, for a few bars, the real thing emerged, the real music, the music that does not die, confident, serene.

I was playing for myself. But at some point a board creaked or a shadow passed across the curtain and I knew he was outside listening.

So I played Bach for him, as well as I could. When the last bar was played I closed the music and sat with my hands in my lap contemplating the oval portrait on the cover with its heavy jowls, its sleek smile, its puffy eyes. Pure spirit, I thought, yet in how unlikely a temple! Where does that spirit find itself now? In the echoes of my fumbling performance receding through the ether? In my heart, where the music still dances? Has it made its way into the heart too of the man in the sagging trousers eavesdropping at the window? Have our two hearts, our organs of love, been tied for this brief while by a cord of sound?

The telephone rang: a woman from the flats across the road warning me of a vagrant she had spied on my property. "He is not a vagrant," I said. "He is a man who works for me."

I am going to stop answering the telephone. There is no one I am ready to speak to except you and the fat man in the picture, the fat man in heaven; and neither of you will, I think, call.

Heaven. I imagine heaven as a hotel lobby with a high ceiling and the Art of Fugue coming softly over the public-address system. Where one can sit in a deep leather armchair and be without pain. A hotel lobby full of old people dozing, listening to the music, while souls pass and repass before them like vapors, the souls of all. A place dense with souls. Clothed? Yes, clothed, I suppose; but with empty hands. A place to which you bring nothing but an abstract kind of clothing and the memories inside you, the memories that make you. A place without incident. A railway station after the abolition of trains. Listening to the heavenly unending music, waiting for nothing, paging idly through the store of memories.

Will it be possible to sit in that armchair listening to the music without fretting about the house closed up and dark, the cats prowling in the garden, unfed, cross? It must be possible, or what is heaven for? Yet dying without succession is— forgive me for saying this—so unnatural. For peace of mind, for peace of soul, we need to know who comes after us, whose presence fills the rooms we were once at home in.

I think of those abandoned farmhouses I drove past in the Karoo and on the west coast whose owners decamped to the cities years ago, leaving fronts boarded up, gates locked. Now washing flaps on the line, smoke comes from the chimney, children play outside the back door, waving to passing cars. A land in the process of being repossessed, its heirs quietly announcing themselves. A land taken by force, used, despoiled, spoiled, abandoned in its barren late years. Loved too, perhaps, by its ravishers, but loved only in the bloomtime of its youth, and therefore, in the verdict of history, not loved enough.

They open your fingers after the event to make sure you are not trying to take something with you. A pebble. A feather. A mustard seed under your fingernail.

It is like a sum, a labyrinthine sum, pages long, subtraction upon subtraction, division upon division, till the head reels. Every day I attempt it anew, in my heart the flicker of a hope that in this one case, my case, there may have been a mistake. And every day I stop before the same blank wall: death, oblivion. Dr. Syfret in his rooms: "We must face the truth." That is to say: We must face the wall. But not he: I.

I think of prisoners standing on the brink of the trench into which their bodies will tumble. They plead with the firing squad, they weep, they joke, they offer bribes, they offer everything they possess: the rings off their fingers, the clothes off their backs. The soldiers laugh. For they will take it all anyway, and the gold from their teeth too.

There is no truth but the shock of pain that goes through me when, in an unguarded moment, a vision overtakes me of this house, empty, with sunlight pouring through the windows onto an empty bed, or of False Bay under blue skies, pristine, deserted—when the world I have passed my life in manifests itself to me and I am not of it. My existence from day to day has become a matter of averting my eyes, of cringing. Death is the only truth left. Death is what I cannot bear to think. At every moment when I am thinking of something else, I am not thinking death, am not thinking the truth.

I try to sleep. I empty my mind; calm begins to steal over me. I am falling, I think, I am falling: welcome, sweet sleep.

Then at the very edge of oblivion something looms up and pulls me back, something whose name can only be *dread*. I shake myself free. I am awake in my room in my bed, all is well. A fly settles on my cheek. It cleans itself. It begins to explore. It walks across my eye, my open eye. I want to blink, I want to wave it away, but I cannot. Through an eye that is and is not mine, I stare at it. It licks itself, if that is the word. There is nothing in those bulging organs that I can recognize as a face. But it is upon me, it is here: it struts across me, a creature from another world.

Or it is two in the afternoon. I am lying on the sofa or in bed, trying to keep the weight off my hip, where the pain is worst. I have a vision of Esther Williams, of plump girls in flowered bathing costumes swimming in effortless backstroke formation through sky-blue, rippling waters, smiling and singing. Invisible guitars strum; the mouths of the girls, bows of vivid scarlet lipstick, form words. What are they singing? Sunset . . . Farewell . . . Tahiti. Longing sweeps through me for the old Savoy bioscope, for tickets at one and fourpence in a currency gone forever, melted down save for a few last farthings in my desk drawer, on one side George VI, the good king, the stammerer, on the other a pair of nightingales. Nightingales. I have never heard nightingale song and never will. I embrace the longing, embrace the regret, embrace the king, the swimming girls, embrace whatever will occupy me.

Or I get up and switch on the television. On one channel football. On the other a black man clasping his hands over the Bible, preaching to me in a language I cannot even put a name to. This is the door I open to let the world flood in, and this is the world that comes to me. It is like peering down a pipe.

Three years ago I had a burglary (you may remember, I

wrote about it). The burglars took no more than they could carry, but before they left they tipped out every drawer, slashed every mattress, smashed crockery, broke bottles, swept all the food in the pantry onto the floor.

"Why do they behave like this?" I asked the detective in bewilderment. "What good does it do them?"

"It's the way they are," he replied. "Animals."

After that I had bars installed on all the windows. They were fitted by a plump Indian man. After he had screwed the bars into the frames he filled in the head of each screw with glue. "So that they can't be unscrewed," he explained. When he left he said, "Now you are safe," and patted my hand.

"Now you are safe." The words of a zookeeper as he locks the door for the night on some wingless, ineffectual bird. A dodo: the last of the dodos, old, past egg-laying. "Now you are safe." Locked up while hungry predators prowl outside. A dodo quaking in her nest, sleeping with one eye open, greeting the dawn haggard. But safe, safe in her cage, the bars intact, the wires intact: the telephone wire, down which she may cry for help in a last extremity, the television wire, down which comes the light of the world, the aerial wire, which calls in music from the stars.

Television. Why do I watch it? The parade of politicians every evening: I have only to see the heavy, blank faces so familiar since childhood to feel gloom and nausea. The bullies in the last row of school desks, raw-boned, lumpish boys, grown up now and promoted to rule the land. They with their fathers and mothers, their aunts and uncles, their brothers and sisters: a locust horde, a plague of black locusts infesting the country, munching without cease, devouring lives. Why, in a spirit of horror and loathing, do I watch them? Why do I let them into the house? Because the reign of the locust family is the truth of South Africa, and the truth is what makes me sick? Legitimacy they no longer trouble to claim. Reason they have shrugged off. What absorbs them is power and the stupor of power. Eating and talking, munching lives, belching. Slow, heavy-bellied talk. Sitting in a circle, debating ponderously, issuing decrees like hammer blows: death, death, death. Untroubled by the stench. Heavy eyelids, piggish eyes, shrewd with the shrewdness of generations of peasants. Plotting against each other too: slow peasant plots that take decades to mature. The new Africans, pot-bellied, heavy-jowled men on their stools of office: Cetshwayo, Dingane in white skins. Pressing downward: their power in their weight. Huge bull testicles pressing down on their wives, their children, pressing the spark out of them. In their own hearts no spark of fire left. Sluggish hearts, heavy as blood pudding.

And their message stupidly unchanging, stupidly forever the same. Their feat, after years of etymological meditation on the word, to have raised stupidity to a virtue. To stupefy: to deprive of feeling; to benumb, deaden; to stun with amazement. Stupor: insensibility, apathy, torpor of mind. Stupid: dulled in the faculties, indifferent, destitute of thought or feeling. From *stupere,* to be stunned, astounded. A gradient from *stupid* to *stunned* to *astonished,* to be turned to stone. The message: that the message never changes. A message that turns people to stone.

We watch as birds watch snakes, fascinated by what is about to devour us. Fascination: the homage we pay to our death. Between the hours of eight and nine we assemble and they show themselves to us. A ritual manifestation, like the processions of hooded bishops during Franco's war. A thanatophany:

showing us our death. *¡Viva la muerte!* their cry, their threat. Death to the young. Death to life. Boars that devour their offspring. The Boar War.

I say to myself that I am watching not the lie but the space behind the lie where the truth ought to be. But is it true?

I dozed (it is still yesterday I am writing about), read, dozed again. I made tea, put on a record. Bar by bar the Goldberg Variations erected themselves in the air. I crossed to the window. It was nearly dark. Against the garage wall the man was squatting, smoking, the point of his cigarette glowing. Perhaps he saw me, perhaps not. Together we listened.

At this moment, I thought, I know how he feels as surely as if he and I were making love.

Though it came unbidden, though it filled me with distaste, I considered the thought without flinching. He and I pressed breast to breast, eyes closed, going down the old road together. Unlikely companions! Like traveling in a bus in Sicily, pressed face to face, body to body against a strange man. Perhaps that is what the afterlife will be like: not a lobby with armchairs and music but a great crowded bus on its way from nowhere to nowhere. Standing room only: on one's feet forever, crushed against strangers. The air thick, stale, full of sighs and murmurs: *Sorry, sorry.* Promiscuous contact. Forever under the gaze of others. An end to private life.

Across the courtyard he squatted, smoking, listening. Two souls, his and mine, twined together, ravished. Like insects mating tail to tail, facing away from each other, still except for a pulsing of the thorax that might be mistaken for mere breathing. Stillness and ecstasy.

He flicked his cigarette away. A burst of sparks as it hit the ground, then darkness.

This house, I thought. This world. This house, this music. This.

"This is my daughter," I said. "The one I told you about, who lives in America." And through his eyes regarded you in the photograph: a pleasant-faced, smiling woman in her thirties, against a field of green, raising a hand to her hair, which is blown by the wind. Confident. That is what you have now: the look of a woman who has found herself.

"These are their children."

Two little boys in caps and coats and boots and gloves standing to attention beside a snowman, waiting for the shutter to click.

A pause. We were sitting at the kitchen table. I had set tea before him, and Marie biscuits. Marie biscuits: food for old people, for the toothless.

"There is something I would like you to do for me if I die. There are some papers I want to send to my daughter. But after the event. That is the important part. That is why I cannot send them myself. I will do everything else. I will make them up into a parcel with the right stamps on it. All you will have to do will be to hand the parcel over the counter at the post office. Will you do that for me?"

He shifted uncomfortably.

"It is not a favor I would ask if I could help it. But there is no other way. I will not be here."

"Can't you ask someone else?" he said.

"Yes, I can. But I am asking you. These are private papers, private letters. They are my daughter's inheritance. They are all I can give her, all she will accept, coming from this country. I don't want them opened and read by anyone else."

Private papers. These papers, these words that either you read *now* or else will never read. Will they reach you? Have they reached you? Two ways of asking the same question, a question to which I will never know the answer, never. To me this letter will forever be words committed to the waves: a message in a bottle with the stamps of the Republic of South Africa on it, and your name.

"I don't know," said the man, the messenger, playing with his spoon.

He will make no promise. And even if he promises, he will do, finally, what he likes. Last instructions, never enforceable. For the dead are not persons. That is the law: all contracts lapse. The dead cannot be cheated, cannot be betrayed, unless you carry them with you in your heart and do the crime there.

"Never mind," I said. "I had thought of asking you to come in and feed the cats as well. But I will make another arrangement."

What other arrangement? In Egypt they bricked in cats with their dead masters. Is that what I want: yellow eyes padding back and forth, searching for a way out of the dark cave?

"I will have to have them put down," I said. "They are too old to take to a new home."

Like water against a rock my words thudded against his silence.

"I have to do something about them," I said. "I can't do nothing. You would feel the same, in my position."

He shook his head. Not true. Indeed, not true. One winter's night, sooner or later, when the artificial fire in his veins is no longer hot enough to preserve him, he will perish. He will die in a doorway or an alley with his arms hugged across his chest; they will find him with this dog or some other dog by his side, whimpering, licking his face. They will cart him off and the dog will be left behind in the street and that will be the end of that. No arrangements, no bequests, no mausoleum.

"I'll post your parcel for you," he said.

Florence is back, bringing not only the two little girls but her fifteen-year-old son, Bheki.

"Is he going to be staying long, Florence?" I asked. "Is there going to be room for him?"

"If he is not with me he will get into trouble," Florence replied. "My sister cannot look after him anymore. It is very bad in Guguletu, very bad."

So now I have five people in the backyard. Five people, a dog, and two cats. The old woman who lived in a shoe. And didn't know what to do.

When Florence went off at the beginning of the month I assured her I could cope with the housework. But of course I let everything slide, and soon a sour, clammy odor pervaded the upstairs, an odor of cold cream, dirty sheets, talcum powder. Now I had to follow shamefacedly after her as she took stock. Hands on hips, nostrils flaring, spectacles gleaming, she surveyed the evidence of my incompetence. Then she set to work. By the end of the afternoon the kitchen and bathroom were shining, the bedroom was crisp and neat, there was a smell of furniture polish in the air. "Wonderful, Florence," I said, producing the ritual phrases. "I don't know what I would do without you." But of course I do know. I would sink into the indifferent squalor of old age.

Having done my work, Florence turned to her own. She put supper on the stove and took the two little girls up to the bathroom. Watching her wash them, wiping hard behind the ears, between the legs, deft, decisive, impervious to their whines, I thought: What an admirable woman, but how glad I am she is not my mother!

I came upon the boy mooning about in the courtyard. Once I knew him as Digby, now he is Bheki. Tall for his age, with Florence's severe good looks. "I can't believe how you have grown," I said. He gave no answer. No longer the open-faced little boy who, when he came visiting, used to run first of all to the rabbit hutch, haul out the fat white doe, and hug her to his chest. Dissatisfied, no doubt, with being separated from his friends and hidden away with baby sisters in someone's backyard.

"Since when have the schools been closed?" I asked Florence.

"Since last week. All the schools in Guguletu, Langa,

Nyanga. The children have got nothing to do. All they do is run around the streets and get into trouble. It is better that he is here where I can see him."

"He will be restless without any friends."

She shrugged, unsmiling. I do not believe I have ever seen her smile. But perhaps she smiles on her children when she is alone with them.

"Who is this man?" asked Florence.

"His name is Mr. Vercueil," I said. "Vercueil, Verkuil, Verskuil. That's what he says. I have never come across such a name before. I am letting him stay here for a while. He has a dog. Tell the children, if they play with it, not to get it too excited. It is a young dog, it may snap."

Florence shook her head.

"If he gives us trouble I will ask him to leave," I said. "But I can't send him away for things he hasn't done."

A cool, windy day. I sat on the balcony in my dressing gown. Below me in the lawn Vercueil was taking the old mower apart, with the little girls watching him. The elder, whose name, says Florence, is Hope (she does not entrust me with the real name), squatted a few yards away, out of his line of vision, her hands clasped between her knees. She was wearing new red sandals. The baby, Beauty, also wearing red sandals, staggered about the lawn, kicking out her feet, sometimes sitting down suddenly.

As I watched, the baby advanced upon Vercueil, her arms held out wide, her fists clenched. As she was about to stumble over the lawn mower he caught her and led her by the chubby little arm to a safe distance. Again, on unsteady feet, she bore down on him. Again he caught her and led her away. It was on the verge of becoming a game. But would dour Vercueil play?

Once more Beauty lunged toward him; once more he saved her. Then, wonder of wonders, he wheeled the half-dismantled lawn mower to one side and, offering one hand to the baby, one hand to Hope, began to turn in circles, first slowly, then faster. Hope, in her red sandals, had to run to keep her footing; as for the baby, she spun in the air, giving shrieks of pleasure; while the dog, closed off behind the gate, leapt and barked. Such noise! Such excitement!

At that point Florence must have come on the scene, for the spinning slowed and stopped. A few soft words, and Hope let go of Vercueil's hand, coaxed her sister away, disappeared from my sight. I heard a door shut. The dog, full of regret, whined. Vercueil returned to the lawn mower. Half an hour later it began to rain.

The boy, Bheki, spends his time sitting on Florence's bed paging through old magazines, while from a corner of the room Hope watches and worships. Sometimes when he has had enough of reading he stands in the driveway bouncing a tennis ball off the garage door. I find the noise maddening. Though I clutch a pillow over my head the remorseless thudding still reaches me. "When are the schools going to open again?" I ask peevishly. "I will tell him to stop," says Florence. A minute later the thudding stops.

Last year, when the troubles in the schools began, I spoke my mind to Florence. "In my day we considered education a privilege," I said. "Parents would scrimp and save to keep their children in school. We would have thought it madness to burn a school down."

"It is different today," replied Florence.

"Do you approve of children burning down their schools?"

"I cannot tell these children what to do," said Florence. "It is all changed today. There are no more mothers and fathers."

"That is nonsense," I said. "There are always mothers and fathers." On that note our exchange ended.

Of trouble in the schools the radio says nothing, the television says nothing, the newspapers say nothing. In the world they project all the children of the land are sitting happily at their desks learning about the square on the hypotenuse and the parrots of the Amazonian jungle. What I know about events in Guguletu depends solely on what Florence tells me and on what I can learn by standing on the balcony and peering northeast: namely, that Guguletu is not burning today, or, if it is burning, is burning with a low flame.

The country smolders, yet with the best will in the world I can only half-attend. My true attention is all inward, upon the thing, the word, the word for the thing inching through my body. An ignominious occupation, and in times like these ridiculous too, as a banker with his clothes on fire is a joke while a burning beggar is not. Yet I cannot help myself. "Look at me!" I want to cry to Florence: "I too am burning!"

Most of the time I am careful to hold the letters of the word apart like the jaws of a trap. When I read I read warily, jumping over lines or even whole paragraphs when from the corner of an eye I catch the shadow of the word waiting in ambush.

But in the dark, in bed, alone, the temptation to look at it grows too strong. I feel myself almost pushed toward it. I think of myself as a child in a long white dress and straw hat on a great empty beach. Sand flies all around me. I hold my hat tight, I plant my feet, I brace myself against the wind. But after a while, in this lonely place where no one is watching, the effort becomes too great. I relax. Like a hand in the small of my back, the wind gives me a push. It is a relief to stop resisting. First walking, then racing, I allow the wind to take me.

It takes me, night after night, to *The Merchant of Venice.* "Do I not eat, sleep, breathe like you?" cries Shylock the Jew: "Do I not bleed like you?" brandishing a dagger with a pound of bleeding flesh impaled on its point. "Do I not bleed like you?" come the words of the Jew with the long beard and skullcap dancing in rage and anguish on the stage.

I would cry my cry to you if you were here. But you are not. Therefore it must be to Florence. Florence must be the one to suffer these moments when a veritable blast of fear goes out from me scorching the leaf on the bough. "It will be all right": those are the words I want to hear uttered. I want to be held to someone's bosom, to Florence's, to yours, to anyone's, and told that it will be all right.

Lying in bed last night with a pillow under my hip, my arms pressed to my chest to keep the pain from moving, the clock showing 3:45, I thought with envy and yearning of Florence in her room, asleep, surrounded by her sleeping children, the four of them breathing in their four different measures, every breath strong and clean.

Once I had everything, I thought. Now you have everything and I have nothing.

The four breathings went on, without falter, and the soft ticking of the clock.

Folding a sheet of paper in two, I wrote Florence a note: "Am having a bad night. Will try to sleep late. Please keep the children quiet. Thank you. E.C." I went downstairs and propped it in the middle of the kitchen table. Then, shivering, I returned to bed, took the four o'clock pills, closed my eyes, folded my arms, and waited for sleep that did not come.

What I want from Florence I cannot have. Nothing of what I want can I have.

Last year, when the little one was still a babe in arms, I gave Florence a ride out to Brackenfell, to the place where her husband works.

No doubt she expected me to drop her there and drive off. But out of curiosity, wanting to see the man, to see them together, I came in with her.

It was late on a Saturday afternoon. From the parking lot we followed a dusty track past two long, low sheds to a third shed, where a man in blue overalls stood in a wire enclosure with chickens—pullets really—milling around his legs. The girl, Hope, tugged herself free, dashed ahead and gripped the mesh. Between the man and Florence something passed: a glance, a question, a recognition.

But there was no time for greetings. He, William, Florence's husband, had a job and the job could not be interrupted. His job was to pounce on a chicken, swing it upside down, grip the struggling body between his knees, twist a wire band around its legs, and pass it on to a second, younger man, who would hang it, squawking and flapping, on a hook on a clattering overhead conveyor that took it deeper into the shed, where a third man in oilskins splashed with blood gripped its head, drew its neck taut, and cut it through with a knife so small it seemed part of his hand, tossing the head in the same movement into a bin full of other dead heads.

This was William's work, and this I saw before I had the time or the presence of mind to ask whether I wanted to see it. For six days of the week this was what he did. He bound the legs of chickens. Or perhaps he took turns with the other men and hung chickens from hooks or cut off heads. For three hundred rand a month plus rations. A work he had been doing for fifteen years. So that it was not inconceivable that some of the bodies I had stuffed with bread crumbs and egg yolk and sage and rubbed with oil and garlic had been held, at the last, between the legs of this man, the father of Florence's children. Who got up at five in the morning, while I was still asleep, to hose out the pans under the cages, fill the feed troughs, sweep the sheds, and then, after breakfast, begin the slaughtering, the plucking and cleaning, the freezing of thousands of carcasses, the packing of thousands of heads and feet, miles of intestines, mountains of feathers.

I should have left at once, when I saw what was going on. I should have driven off and done my best to forget all about it. But instead I stood at the wire enclosure, fascinated, as the three men dealt out death to the flightless birds. And beside me the child, her fingers gripping the mesh, drank in the sight too.

So hard and yet so easy, killing, dying.

Five o'clock came, the end of the day, and I said good-bye. While I was driving back to this empty house, William took Florence and the children to the living quarters. He washed; she cooked a supper of chicken and rice on the paraffin stove, then fed the baby. It was Saturday. Some of the other farm workers were out visiting, recreating themselves. So Florence and William were able to put the children to bed in an empty bunk and go for a walk, just the two of them, in the warm dusk.

They walked along the side of the road. They spoke about the past week, about how it had been; they spoke about their lives.

When they came back the children were fast asleep. For the sake of privacy they hung a blanket in front of their bunk. Then they had the night to themselves, all save the half hour when Florence slipped out and, in the dark, fed the baby.

On Sunday morning William—not his true name but the name by which he is known in the world of his work—put on his suit and hat and good shoes. He and Florence walked to the bus stop, she with the baby on her back, he holding Hope's hand. They took a bus to Kuilsrivier, then a taxi to the home in Guguletu of the sister with whom their son lodged.

It was after ten o'clock and beginning to grow hot. Church was over; the living room was crowded with visitors, full of talk. After a while the men went off; it was time for Florence to help her sister with the cooking. Hope fell asleep on the floor. A dog came in, licked her face, was chased away; she was lifted, still sleeping, onto the sofa. In a private moment Florence gave her sister the money for Bheki's rent, for his food, his shoes, his schoolbooks; her sister put it away in her bodice. Then Bheki made his appearance and greeted his mother. The men came back from wherever they had been and they all had lunch: chicken from the farm or factory or plant or whatever it is, rice, cabbage, gravy. From outside Bheki's friends began to call: hurriedly he finished his food and left the table.

All of this happened. All of this must have happened. It was an ordinary afternoon in Africa: lazy weather, a lazy day. Almost it is possible to say: This is how life should be.

The time came for them to leave. They walked to the bus stop, Hope riding now on her father's shoulders. The bus arrived; they said good-bye. The bus bore Florence and her daughters off. It bore them to Mowbray, from where they took another bus to St. George's Street, and then a third up Kloof Street. From Kloof Street they walked. By the time they reached Schoonder Street the shadows were lengthening. It was time to give Hope, fretful and tired, her supper, to bathe the baby, to finish yesterday's ironing.

At least it is not cattle he is slaughtering, I told myself; at least it is only chickens, with their crazy chicken-eyes and their delusions of grandeur. But my mind would not leave the farm, the factory, the *enterprise* where the husband of the woman who lived side by side with me worked, where day after day he bestrode his pen, left and right, back and forth, around and around, in a smell of blood and feathers, in an uproar of outraged squawking, reaching down, scooping up, gripping, binding, hanging. I thought of all the men across the breadth of South Africa who, while I sat gazing out of the window, were killing chickens, moving earth, barrowful upon barrowful; of all the women sorting oranges, sewing buttonholes. Who would ever count them, the spadefuls, the oranges, the buttonholes, the chickens? A universe of labor, a universe of counting: like sitting in front of a clock all day, killing the seconds as they emerged, counting one's life away.

Ever since Vercueil took my money he has been drinking steadily, drinking not only wine but brandy. Some days he does not drink till noon, using the hours of abstinence to make surrender more voluptuous. More often he is intoxicated by the time he leaves the house in midmorning.

The sun was shining bleakly today when he returned from his outing. I was upstairs on the balcony; he did not see me as he sat down in the yard with his back to the wall, the dog beside him. Florence's son was already there, with a friend I had not seen before, and Hope, devouring their every move with her eyes. They had a radio on; the scraping and thudding of the music was even worse than the tennis ball.

"Water," Vercueil called to the boys. "Bring me some water."

The new boy, the friend, crossed the yard and squatted beside him. What passed between them I did not hear. The boy stretched out a hand. "Give," he said.

Lazily Vercueil beat down his hand.

"Give it to me," the boy said, and on his knees began to tug the bottle from Vercueil's pocket.

Vercueil resisted, but only lackadaisically.

The boy unscrewed the cap and poured the brandy out onto the ground. Then he tossed the bottle aside. It shattered. A stupid thing to do: I almost called out.

"They are making you into a dog!" said the boy. "Do you want to be a dog?"

The dog, Vercueil's dog, whined eagerly.

"Go to hell," replied Vercueil with a thick tongue.

"Dog!" said the boy. "Drunkard!"

He turned his back on Vercueil and went back to Bheki, a swagger in his walk. What a self-important child, I thought. If this is how the new guardians of the people conduct themselves, Lord spare us from them.

The little girl sniffed at the brandy and wrinkled her nose.

"You go to hell too," said Vercueil, waving her away. She did not stir. Then at once she turned and ran to her mother's room.

The music ground on. Vercueil fell asleep, slumped sideways against the wall with the dog's head on his knee. I returned to my book. After a while the sun went behind the clouds and it grew chilly. A light drizzle began to fall. The dog shook itself and went into the shed. Vercueil got to his feet and followed. I gathered my things.

Inside the shed there was a commotion. First the dog scuttled out, faced around, and stood barking; then Vercueil emerged backward; then the two boys followed. As the second boy, the friend, neared him, Vercueil struck out and hit him on the neck with the flat of his hand. The boy drew in his breath with a hiss of surprise: even from the balcony I heard it. He struck back at Vercueil, who stumbled and nearly fell. The dog danced around, yapping. The boy struck Vercueil again, and now Bheki joined in. "Stop it!" I shouted down at them. They paid me no heed. Vercueil was on the ground; they were kicking him; Bheki took out the belt from his trousers and began to lash him. "Florence!" I shouted. "Stop them!" Vercueil put his hands over his face to protect himself. The dog made a leap at Bheki; Bheki knocked it backward and went on flailing Vercueil with his belt. "Stop it, you two!" I shouted, gripping the rail. "Stop it at once or I'll call the police!"

Then Florence appeared. She spoke sharply, and the boys backed off. Vercueil struggled to his feet. I came downstairs as fast as I could.

"Who is this boy?" I asked Florence.

The boy stopped speaking to Bheki and regarded me. I did not like that look: arrogant, combative.

"He is a friend from school," said Florence.

"He must go home," I said. "This is getting too much for me. I can't have brawling in my backyard. I can't have strangers walking in and out."

There was blood coming from Vercueil's lip. Strange to see blood on that leathery face. Like honey on ashes.

"He is not a stranger, he is visiting," said Florence.

"Must we have a pass to come in here?" said Bheki. He and his friend exchanged glances. "Must we have a pass?" They waited for my answer, challenging me. The radio was still playing: an inhuman noise, wearying: I wanted to clasp my hands over my ears.

"I did not say anything about passes," I said. "But what right does he have to come here and assault this man? This man lives here. It is his home."

Florence's nostrils flared.

"Yes," I said, turning to her, "he lives here too, it is his home."

"He lives here," said Florence, "but he is rubbish. He is good for nothing."

"Jou moer!" said Vercueil. He had taken off his hat and was punching out the crown; now he raised the hand with the hat as if to strike her. *"Jou moer!"*

Bheki snatched the hat from him and tossed it up onto the garage roof. The dog barked furiously. Slowly the hat tumbled down the slope of the roof.

"He is not a rubbish person," I said, lowering my voice, speaking to Florence alone. "There are no rubbish people. We are all people together."

But Florence had no desire to be preached to. "Good for nothing but drinking," she said. "Drink, drink, drink all day. I do not like him here."

A good-for-nothing: was that what he was? Yes, perhaps: good-for-nothing: a good old English word, heard too seldom nowadays.

"He is my messenger," I said.

Florence regarded me suspiciously.

"He is going to carry messages for me," I said.

She shrugged. Vercueil shambled off with his hat and his dog. I heard the gate latch click. "Tell the boys to leave him alone," I said. "He is doing no harm."

Like an old tom chased off by the rising males, Vercueil has gone into hiding to lick his wounds. I foresee myself searching the parks, calling softly, "Mr. Vercueil! Mr. Vercueil!" An old woman in search of her cat.

Florence is openly proud of how Bheki got rid of the good-for-nothing, but predicts that he will be back as soon as it starts raining. As for me, I doubt we will see him as long as the boys are here. I said so to Florence. "You are showing Bheki and his friends that they can raise their hands against their elders with impunity. That is a mistake. Yes, whatever you may think of him, Vercueil is their elder!

"The more you give in, Florence, the more outrageously the children will behave. You told me you admire your son's generation because they are afraid of nothing. Be careful: they may start by being careless of their own lives and end by being careless of everyone else's. What you admire in them is not necessarily what is best.

"I keep thinking of what you said the other day: that there are no more mothers and fathers. I can't believe you meant it. Children cannot grow up without mothers or fathers. The burnings and killings one hears of, the shocking callousness, even this matter of beating Mr. Vercueil—whose fault is it in the end? Surely the blame must fall on parents who say, 'Go, do as you wish, you are your own master now, I give up authority over you.' What child in his heart truly wants to be told that? Surely he will turn away in confusion, thinking to himself, 'I have no mother now, I have no father: then let my mother be death, let my father be death.' You wash your hands of them and they turn into the children of death."

Florence shook her head. "No," she said firmly.

"But do you remember what you told me last year, Florence, when those unspeakable things were happening in the townships? You said to me, 'I saw a woman on fire, burning, and when she screamed for help, the children laughed and threw more petrol on her.' You said, 'I did not think I would live to see such a thing.' "

"Yes, I did say that, and it is true. But who made them so cruel? It is the whites who made them so cruel! Yes!" She breathed deeply, passionately. We were in the kitchen. She was doing the ironing. The hand that held the iron pressed down hard. She glared at me. Lightly I touched her hand. She raised the iron. On the sheet was the beginning of a brown scorch mark.

No mercy, I thought: a war without mercy, without limits. A good war to miss.

"And when they grow up one day," I said softly, "do you think the cruelty will leave them? What kind of parents will they become who were taught that the time of parents is over?

Can parents be recreated once the idea of parents has been destroyed within us? They kick and beat a man because he drinks. They set people on fire and laugh while they burn to death. How will they treat their own children? What love will they be capable of? Their hearts are turning to stone before our eyes, and what do you say? You say, 'This is not my child, this is the white man's child, this is the monster made by the white man.' Is that all you can say? Are you going to blame them on the whites and turn your back?"

"No," said Florence. "That is not true. I do not turn my back on my children." She folded the sheet crosswise and lengthwise, crosswise and lengthwise, the corners falling together neatly, decisively. "These are good children, they are like iron, we are proud of them." On the board she spread the first of the pillow slips. I waited for her to say more. But there was no more. She was not interested in debating with me.

Children of iron, I thought. Florence herself, too, not unlike iron. The age of iron. After which comes the age of bronze. How long, how long before the softer ages return in their cycle, the age of clay, the age of earth? A Spartan matron, iron-hearted, bearing warrior sons for the nation. "We are proud of them." We. Come home either with your shield or on your shield.

And I? Where is my heart in all of this? My only child is thousands of miles away, safe; soon I will be smoke and ash; so what is it to me that a time has come when childhood is despised, when children school each other never to smile, never to cry, to raise fists in the air like hammers? Is it truly a time out of time, heaved up out of the earth, misbegotten, monstrous? What, after all, gave birth to the age of iron but the age of granite? Did we not have Voortrekkers, generation after generation of Voortrekkers, grim-faced, tight-lipped Afrikaner children, marching, singing their patriotic hymns, saluting their flag, vowing to die for their fatherland? *Ons sal lewe, ons sal sterwe.* Are there not still white zealots preaching the old regime of discipline, work, obedience, self-sacrifice, a regime of death, to children some too young to tie their own shoelaces? What a nightmare from beginning to end! The spirit of Geneva triumphant in Africa. Calvin, black-robed, thin-blooded, forever cold, rubbing his hands in the afterworld, smiling his wintry smile. Calvin victorious, reborn in the dogmatists and witch-hunters of both armies. How fortunate you are to have put all this behind you!

The other boy, Bheki's friend, arrived on a red bicycle with fat sky-blue tires. When I went to bed last night the bicycle was in the courtyard, glistening wet in the moonlight. At seven this morning, when I looked out of the window, it was still there. I took the morning pills and had another hour's sleep. I dreamed I was trapped in a crowd. Shapes pushed at me, hit at me, swore in words I could not make out, filthy, full of menace. I hit back, but my arms were a child's arms: *foo, foo* went my blows, like puffs of air.

I awoke to the sound of raised voices, Florence's and someone else's. I rang the bell once, twice, three times, four times. At last Florence came.

"Is there someone at the door, Florence?"

Florence picked up the quilt from the floor and folded it over the foot of the bed. "It is nobody," she said.

"Did your son's friend stay here last night?"

"Yes. He cannot ride a bicycle in the dark, it is too dangerous."

"And where did he sleep?"

Florence drew herself up. "In the garage. Bheki and he slept in the garage."

"But how did they get into the garage?"

"They opened the window."

"Can't they ask me before they do something like that?"

A silence. Florence picked up the tray.

"Is this boy going to be living here too, in the garage? Are they sleeping in my car, Florence?"

Florence shook her head. "I do not know. You must ask them yourself."

Midday, and the bicycle was still here. Of the boys themselves no sign. But when I went out to the mailbox there was a yellow police van parked across the street with two uniformed men in it, the one on the near side asleep, his cheek against the glass.

I beckoned to the man behind the wheel. The engine came to life, the sleeper sat up, the van climbed the sidewalk, made a brisk U-turn, and pulled up beside me.

I expected them to get out. But no, there they sat without a word, waiting for me to speak. A cold northwester was blowing. I held my dressing gown closed at my throat. The radio in the van crackled. *"Vier-drie-agt,"* said a woman's voice. They ignored it. Two young men in blue.

"Can I help you?" I said. "Are you waiting for someone?"

"Can you help us? I don't know, lady. You tell us, can you help us."

In my day, I thought, policemen spoke respectfully to

ladies. In my day children did not set fire to schools. *In my day:* a phrase one came across in this day only in letters to the editor. Old men and women, trembling with just fury, taking up the pen, weapon of last resort. In my day, now over; in my life, now past.

"If you are looking for those boys, I want you to know they have my permission to be here."

"Which boys, lady?"

"The boys who are visiting here. The boys from Guguletu. The schoolboys."

There was a burst of noise from the radio.

"No, lady, I don't know anything about boys from Guguletu. Do you want us to look out for them?"

A glance passed between the two of them, a glance of merriment. I gripped the bar of the gate. The dressing gown gaped, I felt the cold wind on my throat, my chest. "In my day," I said, enunciating clearly each old, discredited, comical word, "a policeman did not speak to a lady like that." And I turned my back on them.

The radio squawked like a parrot behind me; or perhaps they made the sound come from it, I would not put it past them. An hour later the yellow van was still outside the gate.

"I really think you should send this other boy home," I told Florence. "He is going to get your son into trouble."

"I cannot send him home," said Florence. "If he goes Bheki will go with him. They are like this." She held up a hand, two fingers intertwined. "It is safer for them here. In Guguletu there is trouble all the time, and then the police come in and shoot."

Shooting in Guguletu: whatever Florence knows about it, whatever you know ten thousand miles away, I do not know.

In the news that reaches me there is no mention of trouble, of shooting. The land that is presented to me is a land of smiling neighbors.

"If they are here to get away from the fighting then why are the police after them?"

Florence drew a deep breath. Since the birth of the baby there has been an air of barely contained outrage about her. "You must not ask *me*, madam," she declared, "why the police are coming after the children and chasing them and shooting them and putting them in jail. You must not ask *me*."

"Very well," I said, "I will not make that mistake again. But I cannot turn my home into a haven for all the children running away from the townships."

"But why not?" asked Florence, leaning forward. "Why not?"

I ran a hot bath, undressed, and painfully lowered myself into the water. *Why not?* I hung my head; the ends of my hair, falling over my face, touched the water; my legs, mottled, blue-veined, stuck out like sticks before me. An old woman, sick and ugly, clawing on to what she has left. The living, impatient of long dyings; the dying, envious of the living. An unsavory spectacle: may it be over soon.

No bell in the bathroom. I cleared my throat and called: "Florence!" Bare pipes and white walls gave back a hollow sound. Absurd to imagine that Florence would hear me. And if she heard, why should she come?

Dear mother, I thought, look down on me, stretch forth your hand!

Shivers began to run through me from head to toe. Behind closed eyes I saw my mother as she is when she appears to me, in her drab old person's clothes, her face hidden.

"Come to me!" I whispered.

But she would not. Stretching out her arms as a coasting hawk does, my mother began to ascend into the sky. Higher and higher she rose above me. She reached the layer of the clouds, pierced it, soared on. With each mile she ascended she became younger. Her hair grew dark again, her skin fresh. The old clothes fell from her like dry leaves, revealing the blue dress with the feather in the buttonhole that she wears in my earliest memory of her, from the time when the world was young and all things were possible.

On she soared, in the eternal perfection of youth, change-less, smiling, rapt, forgetful, to the rim of the heavenly sphere itself. "Mother, look down on me!" I whispered into the bare bathroom.

The rains began early this year. This is the fourth month of rain. Where one touches the walls, streaks of damp form. There are patches where the plaster is blistering and bursting. My clothes have a bitter, moldy smell. How I long, just once more, to put on crisp underwear smelling of the sun! Let me be granted just one more summer-afternoon walk down the Avenue amid the nut-brown bodies of children on their way home from school, laughing, giggling, smelling of clean young sweat, the girls every year more beautiful, *plus belles*. And if that is not to be, let there still be, to the last, gratitude, unbounded, heartfelt gratitude, for having been granted a spell in this world of wonders.

I write these words sitting in bed, my knees pressed together against the August cold. *Gratitude:* I write down the word and read it back. What does it mean? Before my eyes it grows dense, dark, mysterious. Then something happens. Slowly, like a pomegranate, my heart bursts with gratitude; like a fruit splitting open to reveal the seeds of love. *Gratitude, pomegranate:* sister words.

At five this morning I was woken by heavy rain. It came down in sheets, streaming over the edges of the clogged gutters, dripping through cracked roof tiles. I went downstairs, made myself tea, and, wrapped in a blanket, settled down with the month's accounts.

The gate clicked and steps came up the driveway. A figure crouched under a black plastic sack scurried past the window.

I went out onto the veranda. "Mr. Vercueil!" I called into the teeming rain. There was no answer. Hunching my shoulders, clutching the dressing gown about me, I stepped out. At once my slippers with their silly lamb's wool collars were soaked through. Through runnels of water I slopped across the yard. In the dark entrance to the shed I collided with someone: Vercueil, standing with his back to me. He swore.

"Come inside!" I shouted above the rain. "Come into the house! You can't sleep there!"

Still holding the bag like a hood over his head, he followed me into the kitchen and into the light. "Leave that wet thing outside," I said. Then with a shock I saw that someone had followed him in. It was a woman, small, no higher than my shoulder, but old, or at least not young, with a leering, bloated face and livid skin.

"Who is this?" I said.

Vercueil stared back at me, yellow-eyed, defiant. Dog-man! I thought.

"You can wait indoors till the rain stops, then I want you out," I said coldly, and turned my back on the pair of them.

I changed my clothes, locked myself in my bedroom, and tried to read. But the words rustled past me like leaves. With mild surprise I felt my eyelids droop, heard the book slide through my hands.

When I awoke the one thought in my mind was to get them out of the house.

Of the woman there was no sign; but Vercueil was asleep in the living room, curled up on the sofa, his hands between his knees, the hat still somehow on his head. I shook him. He stirred, wet his lips, made a reluctant, mumbling, sleepy sound. It was the same sound—it came back to me at once—that you used to make when I woke you for school. "Time to get up!" I would call as I drew open the curtains; and, turning away from the light, you would mumble just like that. "Come, my darling, it's time to get up!" I would whisper in your ear, not urging you too hard yet, giving myself time to sit beside you and stroke your hair, stroke after stroke, my fingertips alive with love, while you clung to the last to the body of sleep. Let it be like this forever! I would think, my hand on your head, the current of love coursing through it.

And now your sleepy, comfortable murmur reborn in the throat of this man! Should I sit beside him too, lift off his hat, stroke his greasy hair? A shudder of distaste went through me. How easy it is to love a child, how hard to love what a child turns into! Once upon a time, with his fists to his ears and his eyes pinched shut in ecstasy, this creature too floated in a woman's womb, drank of her blood, belly to belly. He too passed through the gates of bone into the radiance outside, was allowed to know mother-love, *amor matris*. Then in the course of time was weaned away from it, made to stand alone, and began to grow dry, stunted, crooked. A life apart, deprived, like all lives; but in this case, surely, more undernourished than most. A man in his middle years still sucking on bottles, yearning for the original bliss, reaching for it in his stupors.

While I stood regarding him, his woman entered the room. Ignoring me, she stumbled back into a nest of cushions on the floor. She reeked of cologne water: mine. Behind her came Florence, bristling.

"Don't ask me to explain, Florence," I said. "Just leave them alone, they are sleeping something off."

Florence's glasses flashed, she had something to say, but I cut her short. "Please! They are not going to stay."

Though I flushed the toilet several times, a smell lingered, both sickly sweet and foul. I tossed the floor mat out in the rain.

Later, when the children were in the kitchen with Florence having breakfast, I came downstairs again. Without preamble I addressed Bheki.

"I hear you and your friend have been sleeping in my car. Why didn't you ask my permission?"

Silence fell. Bheki did not look up. Florence went on cutting bread.

"Why didn't you ask my permission? Answer me!"

The little girl stopped chewing, stared at me.

Why was I behaving in this ridiculous fashion? Because I was irritated. Because I was tired of being used. Because it was my car they were sleeping in. My car, my house: mine; I was not yet gone.

Then, fortunately, Vercueil made his appearance and the tension was broken. He passed through the kitchen, glancing neither left nor right, and out onto the veranda. I followed. The dog was leaping up at him, bounding, frisking, full of joy. It leapt at me too, streaking my skirt with its wet paws. How silly one looks fending off a dog!

"Will you get your friend out of the house, please," I said to him.

Staring up into an overcast sky, he made no reply.

"Get her out at once or I will get her out!" I shouted in a fury.

He ignored me.

"Help me," I ordered Florence.

The woman lay face down on her bed of cushions, a patch of wetness at the corner of her mouth. Florence tugged her by the arm. Groggily she stood up. Half guiding, half pushing, Florence propelled her out of the house. On the pathway Vercueil caught up with us. "This is too much!" I snapped at him.

The two boys were already out on the street with their bicycle. Pretending not to notice our squabble, they set off up Schoonder Street, Bheki hunched on the crossbar, his friend pedaling.

In a hoarse voice, in a rambling stream of obscenity, the woman began to curse Florence. Florence gave me a malicious look. "Rubbish person," she said, and stamped off.

"I don't ever want to see this woman again," I said to Vercueil.

The bicycle with the two boys on it reappeared over the crest of Schoonder Street and raced toward us, Bheki's friend pedaling hard. On their heels followed the yellow police van from yesterday.

A light truck stood parked at the curbside, with pipes and

rods in the back, plumbing materials. There was room enough for the bicycle to pass. But as the yellow van drew level with the boys, the near-side door swung open and slapped them sideways. The bicycle wobbled and went out of control. I had a glimpse of Bheki sliding down, his arms above his head, of the other boy standing on the pedals, averting his face, stretching out a hand in a warding gesture. Above the sound of the traffic from Mill Street I heard quite clearly the thud of a body stopped in midflight, a deep, surprised "Ah!" of exhaled breath, the crash of the bicycle colliding with the plumber's truck. "God!" I screamed in a shrill voice that, hanging in the air, I did not recognize as my own. Time seemed to stop and then resume, leaving a gap: in one instant the boy put out a hand to save himself, in the next he was part of a tangle in the gutter. Then the echo of my scream dwindled and the scene reassembled itself in all its familiarity: Schoonder Street on a quiet weekday morning, with a canary-yellow van just turning the corner.

A dog, a retriever, came trotting up to investigate. Vercueil's dog sniffed the retriever, while the retriever, ignoring him, sniffed the pavement, then began to lick at it. I wanted to move but could not. There was a coldness in me, my limbs felt distant, the word *fainting* occurred to me, though I have never fainted in my life. *This country!* I thought. And then: *Thank God she is out!*

A gate opened and a man in blue work clothes appeared. He kicked at the retriever, which sprang away in hurt surprise. "Jesus!" said the man. He bent down and began to thread limbs through the frame of the bicycle.

I approached, shaking. "Florence!" I called. But there was no sign of Florence.

Straddling the bodies, the man lifted the bicycle aside. Bheki lay under the other boy. There was a deep frown on his face; he wet his lips with his tongue over and over; his eyes were closed. Vercueil's dog tried to lick him. "Go away!" I whispered, and gave it a push with my foot. It wagged its tail.

A woman appeared at my elbow, drying her hands on a towel. "Are they newspaper boys?" she said. "Are they newspaper boys, do you know?" I shook my head.

With an uncertain air, the man in blue straddled the bodies again. What he should have done was to lift the dead weight of the other boy, who lay face down across Bheki. But he did not want to, nor did I want him to. There was something wrong, something unnatural in the way the boy lay.

"I'll go and phone for an ambulance," said the woman.

I bent and raised the boy's limp arm. "Wait!" said the man. "Let's be careful."

Coming erect, I was overtaken with such dizziness that I had to close my eyes.

Clasping him under the shoulders, he dragged the boy off Bheki and laid him out on the pavement. Bheki opened his eyes.

"Bheki," I said. Bheki gave me a calm, incurious look. "Everything is all right," I said. From entirely peaceful eyes he continued to regard me, accepting the lie, letting it pass. "The ambulance is on its way," I said.

Then Florence was there, kneeling beside her son, speaking to him urgently, stroking his head. He began to reply: slow, mumbled words. Her hand paused as she listened. "They crashed into the back of this truck," I explained. "It's my truck," said the man in blue. "The police pushed them," I said. "It's appalling, quite appalling. It was those same two policemen who were here yesterday, I am sure."

Florence slid a hand under Bheki's head. Slowly he sat up. One shoe was off; a trouser leg was torn open and wet with blood. Gingerly he held aside the torn material and peered at the wound. His palms were raw, the skin hung in strips. "The ambulance is on its way," I said. "We do not need the ambulance," said Florence.

She was wrong. The other boy lay sprawled on his back now. With his jacket the plumber was trying to staunch the blood that streamed down his face. But the flow would not stop. He lifted the wadded jacket and for an instant, before it darkened with blood again, I saw that the flesh across the forehead hung open in a loose flap as if sliced with a butcher's knife. Blood flowed in a sheet into the boy's eyes and made his hair glisten; it dripped onto the pavement; it was everywhere. I did not know blood could be so dark, so thick, so heavy. What a heart he must have, I thought, to pump that blood and go on pumping!

"Is the ambulance coming?" said the plumber. "Because I don't know how to stop this." He was sweating; he changed position and his shoe, soggy with blood, squelched.

You were eleven, I remember, when you sliced your thumb in the bread machine. I rushed you to the emergency section at Groote Schuur. We sat on a bench waiting our turn, you with your thumb wrapped in lint, pressing it to stop the bleeding. "What's going to happen to me?" you whispered. "They will give you an injection and put in stitches," I whispered back. "Just a few stitches, just a few pricks."

It was early on a Saturday evening, but already the casualties were trickling in. A man in white shoes and a rumpled black suit spat blood steadily into a dish. A youth on a stretcher, naked to the waist, his belt open, held a wad of sodden cloth to his belly. Blood on the floor, blood on the benches. What did our timid thimbleful count for beside this torrent of black blood? Child Snowdrop lost in the cavern of blood, and her mother lost too. A country prodigal of blood. Florence's husband in yellow oilskins and boots, wading through blood. Oxen keeling over, their throats slit, hurling last jets into the air like whales. The dry earth soaking up the blood of its creatures. A land that drinks rivers of blood and is never sated.

"Let me," I said to the plumber. He made way. Kneeling, I lifted aside the sodden blue jacket. Blood ran down the boy's face in a steady, even sheet. Between thumbs and forefingers I pinched together as much as I could of the open flap. Vercueil's dog came pushing in again. "Get that dog away," I snapped. The plumber gave it a kick. It yelped and sidled away. Where was Vercueil? Was it true, was he truly good for nothing? "Go and phone again," I ordered the plumber.

As long as I pinched tight I could hold in most of the flow. But when I relaxed blood poured again steadily. It was blood, nothing more, blood like yours and mine. Yet never before had I seen anything so scarlet and so black. Perhaps it was an effect of the skin, youthful, supple, velvet dark, over which it ran; but even on my hands it seemed both darker and more glaring than blood ought to be. I stared at it, fascinated, afraid, drawn into a veritable stupor of staring. Yet it was impossible, in my deepest being impossible, to give myself up to that stupor, to relax and do nothing to stop the flow. Why? I ask myself now. And I answer: Because blood is precious, more precious than gold and diamonds. Because blood is one: a pool of life dispersed among us in separate existences, but belonging by nature together: lent, not given: held in common, in trust, to be preserved: seeming to live in us, but only seeming, for in truth we live in it.

A sea of blood, come back together: is that how it will be at the end of days? The blood of all: a Baikal Sea scarlet-black under a wintry blue Siberian sky, ice cliffs around it, its snow-white shores lapped by blood, viscous, sluggish. The blood of mankind, restored to itself. A body of blood. Of all mankind? No: in a place apart, in a mud-walled dam in the Karoo with barbed wire around it and the sun blazing down, the blood of the Afrikaners and their tribute bearers, still, stagnant.

Blood, sacred, abominated. And you, flesh of my flesh, blood of my blood, bleeding every month into foreign soil.

For twenty years I have not bled. The sickness that now eats at me is dry, bloodless, slow and cold, sent by Saturn. There is something about it that does not bear thinking of. To have fallen pregnant with these growths, these cold, obscene swellings; to have carried and carried this brood beyond any natural term, unable to bear them, unable to sate their hunger: children inside me eating more every day, not growing but bloating, toothed, clawed, forever cold and ravenous. Dry, dry: to feel them turning at night in my dry body, not stretching and kicking as a human child does but changing their angle, finding a new place to gnaw. Like insect eggs laid in the body of a host, now grown to grubs and implacably eating their host away. My eggs, grown within me. *Me, mine:* words I shudder to write, yet true. My daughters death, sisters to you, my daughter life. How terrible when motherhood reaches a point of parodying itself! A crone crouched over a boy, her hands sticky with his blood: a vile image, as it comes up in me now.

I have lived too long. Death by fire the only decent death left. To walk into the fire, to blaze like tow, to feel these secret sharers cringe and cry out too, at the last instant, in their harsh unused little voices; to burn and be gone, to be rid of, to leave the world clean. Monstrous growths, misbirths: a sign that one is beyond one's term. This country too: time for fire, time for an end, time for what grows out of ash to grow.

When the ambulance came I was so stiff that I had to be lifted to my feet. In detaching my sticky fingers from the gash I opened it again. "He has lost a lot of blood," I said. "It's not serious," said the ambulance man curtly. He held the boy's eyelid open. "Concussed," he said. "How did it happen?"

Bheki sat on the bed, his trousers off, his hands in a basin of water; Florence knelt before him, bandaging his leg.

"Why did you leave me alone to look after him? Why didn't you stay and help?"

I sounded querulous, certainly, but for once was I not in the right?

"I do not want to be involved with the police," said Florence.

"That is not the question. You leave me alone to take care of your son's friend. Why must I be the one to take care of him? He is nothing to me."

"Where is he?" said Bheki.

"They took him to Woodstock Hospital. He is concussed."

"What does it mean, concussed?"

"He is unconscious. He hit his head. Do you know why you crashed?"

"They pushed us," he said.

"Yes, they pushed you. I saw it. You are lucky to be alive, both of you. I am going to lay a complaint."

A glance passed between Bheki and his mother. "We do not want to be involved with the police," Florence repeated. "There is nothing you can do against the police." Again a glance, as though checking she had her son's approval.

"If you don't complain they will go on behaving as they like. Even if it gets you nowhere, you must stand up to them. I am not talking about the police only. I am talking about men in power. They must see you are not afraid. This is a serious matter. They could have killed you, Bheki. What have they got against you anyway? What have you and that friend of yours been up to?"

Florence knotted the bandage around his leg and murmured something to him. He took his hands out of the basin. There was a smell of antiseptic.

"Is it bad?" I said.

He held out his hands, palms upward. Blood continued to ooze from the raw flesh. Honorable wounds? Would these count on the roll as honorable wounds, wounds of war? Together we regarded the bleeding hands. I had the impression he was holding back tears. A child, no more than a child, playing on a bicycle.

"Your friend," I said. "Don't you think his parents should know?"

"I can phone," said Florence.

Florence telephoned. A long, loud conversation. "Woodstock Hospital," I heard.

Hours later there was a call from a public telephone, a woman wanting Florence.

"He is not in the hospital," Florence reported.

"Was that his mother?" I asked.

"His grannie."

I telephoned Woodstock Hospital. "You won't have his name, he was unconscious when they took him," I said.

"No record of such a patient," said the man.

"He had a terrible gash across the forehead."

"No record," he repeated. I gave up.

"They work with the police," said Bheki. "They are all the same, the ambulances, the doctors, the police."

"That is nonsense," I said.

"Nobody trusts the ambulance anymore. They are always talking to the police on their radios."

"Nonsense."

He smiled a smile not without charm, relishing this chance to lecture me, to tell me about real life. I, the old woman who lived in a shoe, who had no children and didn't know what to do. "It is true," he said. "Listen and you will hear."

"Why are the police after you?"

"They are not after me. They are after everybody. I have done nothing. But anybody they see they think should be in school, they try to get them. We do nothing, we just say we are not going to school. Now they are waging this terror against us. They are terrorists."

"Why won't you go to school?"

"What is school for? It is to make us fit into the apartheid system."

Shaking my head, I turned to Florence. There was a tight little smile on her lips that she did not bother to hide. Her son was winning hands down. Well, let him. "I am too old for this," I said to her. "I can't believe you want your son out on the streets killing time till apartheid comes to an end. Apartheid is not going to die tomorrow or the next day. He is ruining his future."

"What is more important, that apartheid must be destroyed or that I must go to school?" asked Bheki, challenging me, smelling victory.

"That is not the choice," I answered wearily. But was I right? If that was not the choice, what was the choice? "I will take you to Woodstock," I offered. "But then we must leave at once."

When Florence saw Vercueil waiting, she bridled. But I insisted. "He must come along in case I have trouble with the car," I said.

So I drove them to Woodstock, Vercueil beside me smelling worse than ever, somehow smelling miserable too, Florence and Bheki silent in the back. The car struggled up the gentle slope to the hospital; for once I had the presence of mind to park pointing downhill.

"I tell you, there is no such person here," said the man at the desk. "If you don't believe me, go and look in the wards."

Tired though I was, I trailed through the male wards behind Florence and Bheki. It was the hour of the siesta; doves were calling softly from the trees outside. We saw no black boys with bandaged heads, only old white men in pajamas staring emptily at the ceiling while the radio played soothing music. My secret brothers, I thought: this is where I belong.

"If they didn't bring him here, where would they have taken him?" I asked at the desk.

"Try Groote Schuur."

The parking lot at Groote Schuur was full. For half an hour we sat at the gate with the engine idling, Florence and her son talking softly together, Vercueil blank-eyed, I yawning. Like a sleepy weekend in South Africa, I thought; like taking the family for a drive. We could have played a word game to pass the time, but what chance was there of enlisting those three? Word games, from a past that I alone could look back to with nostalgia, when we of the middle classes, the comfortable classes, passed our Sundays roaming the countryside from beauty spot to beauty spot, bringing the afternoon to a close with tea and scones and strawberry jam and cream in a tea room with a nice view, preferably westward over the sea.

A car came out, we went in. "I'll stay here," said Vercueil.

"Where would someone with concussion be taken?" I asked the clerk.

Down long, crowded corridors we passed looking for ward C-5. We crammed ourselves into a lift with four Muslim women wearing veils, carrying dishes of food. Bheki, self-conscious about his bandaged hands, held them behind his back. Through C-5, through C-6, and no sign of the boy. Florence stopped a nurse. "Try the new wing," she suggested. Exhausted, I shook my head. "I can't walk any further," I said. "You and Bheki go on; I will meet you at the car."

It was true, I was tired, my hip ached, my heart was thumping, there was an unpleasant taste in my mouth. But there was more to it than that. I was seeing too many sick old people, and too suddenly. They oppressed me, oppressed and intimidated me. Black and white, men and women, they shuffled about the corridors, watching each other covetously, eyeing me as I approached, catching unerringly on me the smell of death. "Impostor!" they seemed to whisper, ready to grasp my arm, draw me back. "Do you think you can come and go here as you please? Don't you know the rule? This is the house of shadow and suffering through which you must pass on the way to death. That is the sentence passed upon all: a term in prison before the execution." Old hounds patrolling the corridors, seeing that none of the condemned flee back to the air, the light, the bounteous world above. Hades this place, and I a fugitive shade. I shuddered as I passed through the doorway.

In silence we waited in the car, Vercueil and I, like a couple married too long, talked out, grumpy. I am even getting used to the smell, I thought. Is this how I feel toward South Africa: not loving it but habituated to its bad smell? Marriage is fate. What we marry we become. We who marry South Africa become South Africans: ugly, sullen, torpid, the only sign of life in us a quick flash of fangs when we are crossed. South Africa: a bad-tempered old hound snoozing in the doorway, taking its time to die. And what an uninspired name for a country! Let us hope they change it when they make their fresh start.

A group of nurses passed, laughing, gay, their shift over. It is their ministrations I have been evading, I thought. What a relief it would be to give myself up to them now! Clean sheets, brisk hands on my body, a release from pain, a release into helplessness—what is it that keeps me from yielding? I felt a constriction in my throat, a welling up of tears, and turned my face away. A passing shower, I told myself—English weather. But the truth is, I cry more and more easily, with less and less shame. I knew a woman once (do you mind if your mother talks of these things?) to whom pleasure, orgasm, came very easily. Orgasms would pass through her, she said, like little shudders, one after another, rippling her body like water. How would it be, I used to wonder, to live in a body like that? To be turned to water: is that what bliss is? Now I have an answer of a kind in these flurries of tears, these deliquescences of mine. Tears not of sorrow but of sadness. A light, fickle sadness: the blues, but not the dark blues: the pale blues, rather, of far skies, clear winter days. A private matter, a disturbance of the pool of the soul, which I take less and less trouble to hide.

I dried my eyes, blew my nose. "You needn't be embarrassed," I said to Vercueil. "I cry without reason. Thank you for coming along."

"I don't see what you need me for," he said.

"It is hard to be alone all the time. That's all. I didn't choose you, but you are the one who is here, and that will have to do. You arrived. It's like having a child. You can't choose the child. It just arrives."

Looking away, he gave a slow, crafty smile.

"Besides," I said, "you push the car. If I couldn't use the car I would be trapped at home."

"All you need is a new battery."

"I don't want a new battery. You don't understand that, do you? Do I have to explain? This car is old, it belongs to a world that barely exists anymore, but it works. What is left of that world, what still works, I am trying to hold on to. Whether I love it or hate it does not matter. The fact is, I belong to it as I do not belong, thank God, to what it has become. It is a world in which cars cannot be depended on to start whenever you want them to. In my world you try the self-starter. If that does not work you try the crank handle. If that does not work you get someone to push. And if the car still does not start you get on your bicycle or walk or stay at home. That is how things are in the world where I belong. I am comfortable there, it is a world I understand. I don't see why I should change."

Vercueil said nothing.

"And if you think I am a fossil from the past," I added, "it is time you took a look at yourself. You have seen what the children of today think of drinking and lying around and *leeglopery*. Be warned. In the South Africa of the future everyone will have to work, including you. You may not like the prospect, but you had better prepare yourself for it."

Darkness was falling over the parking lot. Where was Florence? The pain in my back was wearing me down. It was past the time for my pills.

I thought of the empty house, the long night yawning before me. Tears came again, easy tears.

I spoke: "I told you about my daughter in America. My daughter is everything to me. I have not told her the truth, the whole truth about my condition. She knows I was sick, she knows I had an operation; she thinks it was successful and I am getting better. When I lie in bed at night and stare into the black hole into which I am falling, all that keeps me sane is the thought of her. I say to myself: I have brought a child into the world, I have seen her to womanhood, I have seen her safely to a new life: that I have done, that can never be taken from me. That thought is the pillar I cling to when the storms hit me.

"There is a little ritual I go through sometimes that helps me to stay calm. I say to myself: It is two in the morning here, on this side of the world, therefore it is six in the evening there, on her side. Imagine it: six in the evening. Now imagine the rest. Imagine everything. She has just come in from work. She hangs up her coat. She opens the refrigerator and takes out a packet of frozen peas. She empties the peas into a bowl. She takes two onions and begins to peel them. Imagine the peas, imagine the onions. Imagine the world in which she is doing these things, a world with its own smells and sounds. Imagine a summer evening in North America, with gnats at the screen door, children calling from down the street. Imagine my daughter in her house, in her life, with an onion in one hand, in a land where she will live and die in peace. The hours pass, in that land and this one and all the rest of the world, at the same pace. Imagine them passing. They pass: here it grows light, there it grows dark. She goes to bed; drowsily she lies beside the body of her husband in their bed of marriage in their peaceful country. I think of her body, still, solid, alive, at peace, escaped. I ache to embrace her. 'I am so thankful,' I want to say, from a full heart. I also want to say, but never do: 'Save me!'

"Do you understand? Do you understand?"

The car door was open. Vercueil leaned away from me, his head against the doorpost, one foot on the ground. He sighed a heavy sigh; I heard it. Wishing for Florence to return and rescue him, no doubt. How tedious these confessions, these pleas, these demands!

"Because that is something one should never ask of a child," I went on: "to enfold one, comfort one, save one. The comfort, the love should flow forward, not backward. That is a rule, another of the iron rules. When an old person begins to plead for love everything turns squalid. Like a parent trying to creep into bed with a child: unnatural.

"Yet how hard it is to sever oneself from that living touch, from all the touches that unite us with the living! Like a steamer pulling away from the quay, the ribbons tightening, snapping, falling away. Setting off on a last voyage. The dear departed. It is all so sad, so sad! When those nurses passed us a little while ago I was on the point of getting out of the car and giving up, surrendering to the hospital again, letting myself be undressed and put to bed and ministered to by their hands. It is their hands above all that I find myself craving. The touch of hands. Why else do we hire them, these girls, these children, if not to touch, to stroke, in that brisk way of theirs, flesh that has grown old and unlovable? Why do we give them lamps and call them angels? Because they come in the dead of night to tell us it is time to go? Perhaps. But also because they put out a hand to renew a touch that has been broken."

"Tell this to your daughter," said Vercueil quietly. "She will come."

"No."

"Tell her right now. Phone her in America. Tell her you need her here."

"No."

"Then don't tell her afterward, when it is too late. She won't forgive you."

The rebuke was like a slap in the face.

"There are things you don't understand," I said. "I have no intention of summoning my daughter back. I may long for her but I don't want her here. That is why it is called longing. It has to go a long way. To the ends of the earth."

To his credit, he was not deflected by this nonsense. "You have to choose," he said. "Tell her or don't tell her."

"I won't tell her, you can be sure," I said (what a liar I am!). Something was rising in my voice, a tone I could not control. "Let me remind you, this is not a normal country. People can't just come and go as they wish."

He did nothing to help me.

"My daughter will not come back till things have changed

here. She has made a vow. She will not come back to South Africa as you and she and I know it. She will certainly not apply to—what can I call them?—*those people* for permission to come. She will come back when they are hanging by their heels from the lampposts, she says. She will come back then to throw stones at their bodies and dance in the streets."

Vercueil showed his teeth in a broad grin. Yellow horse-teeth. An old horse.

"You don't believe me," I said, "but perhaps one day you will meet her, and then you will see. She is like iron. I am not going to ask her to go back on her vows."

"You are like iron too," he said, to me.

A silence fell between us. Inside me something broke.

"Something broke inside me when you said that," I said, the words just coming. I did not know how to go on. "If I were made of iron, surely I would not break so easily," I said.

The four women we had met in the lift crossed the lot, escorted by a little man in a blue suit and white skullcap. He ushered them into a car and drove them off.

"Did your daughter do something, that she had to leave?" said Vercueil.

"No, she didn't do anything. She had simply had enough. She went away; she didn't come back. She made another life for herself. She got married and started a family. It was the best thing to do, the sensible thing."

"But she hasn't forgotten."

"No, she hasn't forgotten. Though who am I to say? Perhaps one does forget, slowly. I can't imagine it, but perhaps it does happen. She says, 'I was born in Africa, in South Africa.' I have heard her use that phrase in conversation. It sounds to me like the first half of a sentence. There ought to be a second half, but it never comes. So it hangs in the air like a lost twin. 'I was born in South Africa and will never see it again.' 'I was born in South Africa and will one day return.' Which is the lost twin?"

"So she is an exile?"

"No, she is not an exile. I am the exile."

He was learning to talk to me. He was learning to lead me on. I felt an urge to interrupt: "It is such a pleasure!" I wanted to say. After long silence it is such a pleasure: tears come to the eyes.

"I don't know whether you have children. I don't even know whether it is the same for a man. But when you bear a child from your own body you give your life to that child. Above all to the first child, the firstborn. Your life is no longer with you, it is no longer yours, it is with the child. That is why we do not really die: we simply pass on our life, the life that was for a while in us, and are left behind. I am just a shell, as you can see, the shell my child has left behind. It doesn't matter what happens to me. It doesn't matter what happens to old people. Still—I say the words, I cannot expect you to understand, but never mind—it is frightening to be on the edge of leaving. Even if it is only the touch of fingertip to fingertip: one does not want to let go."

Florence and her son were crossing the parking lot now, walking swiftly toward us.

"You should have gone to stay with her," said Vercueil.

I smiled. "I can't afford to die in America," I said. "No one can, except Americans."

Florence got vehemently into the back seat; the car rocked as she settled down.

"Did you find him?" I asked.

"Yes," she replied. Her face was like thunder. Bheki got in beside her.

"And?" I said.

"Yes, we found him, he is in this hospital," said Florence.

"And he is well?"

"Yes, he is well."

"Good," I snapped. "Thank you for telling me."

We drove off in silence. Only when we got home did Florence have her say. "They have put him with the old men in the hospital. It is too terrible. There is one who is mad, who is shouting and swearing all the time, the nurses are afraid to go near him. They should not put a child in a room like that. It is not a hospital where he is, it is a waiting room for the funeral."

A waiting room for the funeral: I could not get the words out of my mind. I tried to eat but had no appetite.

I found Vercueil in the woodshed doing something to a shoe by candlelight. "I am going back to the hospital," I said. "Will you come with me?"

The ward Florence had described was at the far end of the old building, reached by going down to the basement, past the kitchens, then up again.

It was true. A man with a shaven skull, thin as a rake, was sitting up in bed, beating his palms on his thighs and chanting in a loud voice. A broad black strap passed around his middle and under the bed. What was he singing? The words belonged to no tongue I knew of. I stood in the doorway unable to enter, fearing that at any moment he would fix me with his gaze, stop singing, raise one of those skeletal black arms and point.

"DTs," said Vercueil. "He's got the DTs."

"No, it's worse than that," I whispered.

Vercueil took my elbow. I let him lead me in.

There was a long table down the middle of the ward with a jumble of trays on it. Someone was coughing soggily as though his lungs were full of milk. "In the corner," said Vercueil.

He did not know who we were, nor did I easily recognize the boy whose blood had stuck my fingers together. His head was bandaged, his face puffy, his left arm strapped against his chest. He wore pale-blue hospital pajamas.

"Don't talk," I said. "We have just come to make sure you are all right."

He opened the swollen lips and closed them again.

"Do you remember me? I am the woman Bheki's mother works for. I was watching this morning: I saw everything that happened. You must get well quickly. I have brought you some fruit." On the cabinet I placed the fruit: an apple, a pear.

His expression did not change.

I did not like him. I do not like him. I look into my heart and nowhere do I find any trace of feeling for him. As there are people to whom one spontaneously warms, so there are people to whom one is, from the first, cold. That is all. This boy is not like Bheki. He has no charm. There is something stupid about him, something deliberately stupid, obstructive, intractable. He is one of those boys whose voices deepen too early, who by the age of twelve have left childhood behind and turned brutal, knowing. A simplified person, simplified in every way: swifter, nimbler, more tireless than real people, without doubts or scruples, without humor, ruthless, innocent. While he lay in the street, while I thought he was dying, I did what I could for him. But, to be candid, I would rather I had spent myself on someone else.

I remember a cat I once nursed, an old ginger tom whose jaw was locked shut by an abscess. I took him in when he was too weak to resist, fed him milk through a tube, dosed him with antibiotics. When he got back his strength I set him free, but continued to put out food for him. For a year, on and off, I saw him in the neighborhood; for a year the food was taken. Then he vanished for good. In all this time he treated me without compromise as one of the enemy. Even when he was at his weakest his body was hard, tense, resistant under my hand. Around this boy I now felt the same wall of resistance. Though his eyes were open, he did not see; what I said he did not hear.

I turned to Vercueil. "Shall we go?" I said. And on an impulse—no, more than that, with a conscious effort not to block the stirring of the impulse—I touched the boy's free hand.

It was not a clasp, not a long touch; it was the merest brush, the merest lingering of my fingertips on the back of his hand. But I felt him stiffen, felt an angry electric recoil.

For your mother, who is not here, I said within myself. Aloud I said: "Be slow to judge."

Be slow to judge: what did I mean? If I did not know, who else could be expected to? Certainly not he. Yet in his case, I was sure, the incomprehension ran deeper. My words fell off him like dead leaves the moment they were uttered. The words of a woman, therefore negligible; of an old woman, therefore doubly negligible; but above all of a white.

I, a white. When I think of the whites, what do I see? I see a herd of sheep (not a flock: a herd) milling around on a dusty plain under the baking sun. I hear a drumming of hooves, a confusion of sound that resolves itself, when the ear grows attuned, into the same bleating call in a thousand different inflections: "I!" "I!" "I!" And, cruising among them, bumping them aside with their bristling flanks, lumbering, saw-toothed, red-eyed, the savage, unreconstructed old boars grunting "Death!" "Death!" Though it does me no good, I flinch from the white touch as much as he does; would even flinch from the old white woman who pats his hand if she were not I.

I tried again.

"Before I retired," I said, "I was a teacher. I taught at the university."

Vercueil eyed me keenly from the other side of the bed. But I was not talking to him.

"If you had been in my Thucydides class," I went on, "you might have learned something about what can happen to our humanity in time of war. Our humanity, that we are born with, that we are born into."

There was something smoky about the boy's eyes: the whites without luster, the pupils flat, dark, like printer's ink. Though he may have been sedated, he knew I was there, knew who I was, knew I was talking to him. He knew and he did not listen, as he had never listened to any of his teachers, but had sat like a stone in the classroom, impervious to words, waiting for the bell to ring, biding his time.

"Thucydides wrote of people who made rules and followed them. Going by rule they killed entire classes of enemies without exception. Most of those who died felt, I am sure, that a terrible mistake was being made, that, whatever the rule was, it could not be meant for them. 'I!—': that was their last word as their throats were cut. A word of protest: I, the exception.

"Were they exceptions? The truth is, given time to speak, we would all claim to be exceptions. For each of us there is a case to be made. We all deserve the benefit of the doubt.

"But there are times when there is no time for all that close listening, all those exceptions, all that mercy. There is no time, so we fall back on the rule. And that is a great pity, the greatest pity. That is what you could have learned from Thucydides. It is a great pity when we find ourselves entering upon times like those. We should enter upon them with a sinking heart. They are by no means to be welcomed."

Quite deliberately he put his good hand under the sheet, in case I should touch it again.

"Good night," I said. "I hope you sleep well and feel better in the morning."

The old man had stopped chanting. His hands flapped loosely on his thighs like dying fish. His eyes were rolled back, there were streaks of spittle on his chin.

The car would not start, and Vercueil had to push.

"That boy is different from Bheki, quite different," I said, talking too much now, a little out of control. "I try not to show it, but he makes me nervous. I am sorry Bheki has fallen under his influence. But there are hundreds of thousands like him, I suppose. More than there are like Bheki. The rising generation."

We got home. Uninvited, he followed me in.

"I have to sleep, I am exhausted," I said; and then, when he made no move to leave: "Do you want something to eat?"

I put food in front of him, took my pills, waited.

Holding the loaf of bread with his bad hand, he cut a slice, buttered it thickly, cut cheese. His fingernails filthy. Who knows what else he had been touching. And this is the one to whom I speak my heart, whom I trust with last things. Why this crooked path to you?

My mind like a pool, which his finger enters and stirs. Without that finger, stillness, stagnation.

A way of indirection. By indirection I find direction out. A crab's walk.

His dirty fingernail entering me.

"You look gray," he said.

"I am tired."

He chewed, showing long teeth.

He watches but does not judge. Always a faint haze of alcohol about him. Alcohol, that softens, preserves. *Mollificans.* That helps us to forgive. He drinks and makes allowances. His life all allowances. He, Mr. V., to whom I speak. Speak and then write. Speak in order to write. While to the rising generation, who do not drink, I cannot speak, can only lecture. Their hands clean, their fingernails clean. The new puritans, holding to the rule, holding up the rule. Abhorring alcohol, which softens the rule, dissolves iron. Suspicious of all that is idle, yielding, roundabout. Suspicious of devious discourse, like this.

"And I am sick too," I said. "Sick and tired, tired and sick. I have a child inside that I cannot give birth to. Cannot because it will not be born. Because it cannot live outside me. So it is my prisoner or I am its prisoner. It beats on the gate but it cannot leave. That is what is going on all the time. The child inside is beating at the gate. My daughter is my first child. She is my life. This is the second one, the afterbirth, the unwanted. Would you like to watch television?"

"I thought you wanted to sleep?"

"No, I would rather not be alone now. The one inside isn't beating so hard, anyway. He has had his pill, he is getting drowsy. The dose is always two pills, you notice, one for me, one for him."

We sat down side by side on the sofa. A ruddy-faced man was being interviewed. He owned a game farm, it appeared, and rented out lions and elephants to film companies.

"Tell us about some of the overseas personalities you have met," said the interviewer.

"I'm going to make some tea," I said, getting up.

"Is there anything else in the house?" said Vercueil.

"Sherry."

When I returned with the sherry bottle he was standing at the bookshelf. I switched off the television. "What are you looking at?" I asked.

He held up one of the heavy quartos.

"You will find that book interesting," I said. "The woman who wrote it traveled through Palestine and Syria disguised as a man. In the last century. One of those intrepid Englishwomen. But she didn't do the pictures. They were done by a professional illustrator."

Together we paged through the book. By some trick of perspective the illustrator had given to moonlit encampments, desert crags, ruined temples an air of looming mystery. No one has done that for South Africa: made it into a land of mystery. Too late now. Fixed in the mind as a place of flat, hard light, without shadows, without depth.

"Read whatever you like," I said. "There are many more books upstairs. Do you like reading?"

Vercueil put down the book. "I'll go to bed now," he said.

Again a flicker of embarrassment passed across me. Why? Because, to be candid, I do not like the way he smells. Because Vercueil in his underwear I prefer not to think of. The feet worst of all: the horny, caked toenails.

"Can I ask you a question?" I said. "Where did you live before? Why did you start wandering?"

"I was at sea," said Vercueil. "I told you that."

"But one doesn't live at sea. One isn't born at sea. You haven't been at sea all your life."

"I was on trawlers."

"And?"

He shook his head.

"I am just asking," I said. "We like to know a little about the people near to us. It's quite natural."

He gave that crooked smile of his in which one canine suddenly reveals itself, long and yellow. You are hiding something, I thought, but what? A tragic love? A prison sentence? And I broke into a smile myself.

So we stood smiling, the two of us, each with our private cause to smile.

"If you prefer," I said, "you can sleep on the sofa again."

He looked dubious. "The dog is used to sleeping with me."

"You didn't have the dog with you last night."

"He will carry on if I don't come."

I heard no carrying on by the dog last night. As long as he feeds it, does the dog really care where he sleeps? I suspect he uses the fiction of the anxious dog as other men use the fiction of the anxious wife. On the other hand, perhaps it is because of the dog that I trust him. Dogs, which sniff out what is good, what evil: patrollers of boundaries: sentries.

The dog has not warmed to me. Too much cat smell. Cat-woman: Circe. And he, after roaming the seas in trawlers, making landfall here.

"As you please," I said, and let him out, pretending not to notice he still had the sherry bottle.

A pity, I thought (my last thought before the pills took me away): we could set up house, the two of us, after a fashion, I upstairs, he downstairs, for this last little while. So that there will be someone at hand in the nights. For that is, after all, what one wants in the end: someone to be there, to call to in the dark. Mother, or whoever is prepared to stand in for mother.

Since I had declared to Florence I would do so, I visited Caledon Square and tried to lay a charge against the two policemen. But laying a charge, it appears, is permitted only to "parties directly affected."

"Give us the particulars and we will investigate," said the desk officer. "What are the names of the two boys?"

"I can't give you their names without their permission."

He put down his pen. A young man, very neat and correct, one of the new breed of policeman. Whose training is rounded off with a stint in Cape Town to strengthen their self-control in the face of liberal-humanist posturing.

"I don't know whether you take any pride in that uniform," I said, "but your colleagues on the street are disgracing it. They are also disgracing me. I am ashamed. Not for them: for myself. You won't let me lay a charge because you say I am not affected. But I am affected, very directly affected. Do you understand what I am saying?"

He did not reply, but stood stiffly erect, wary, ready for whatever might come next. The man behind him bent over his papers, pretending not to listen. But there was nothing to fear. I had no more to say, or at least not the presence of mind to think of more.

Vercueil sat in the car in Buitenkant Street. "I made such a fool of myself," I said, suddenly on the edge of tears again. " 'You make me feel ashamed,' I told them. They are probably still laughing among themselves. *Die ou kruppel dame met die kaffertjies.* Yet how else can one feel? Perhaps I should simply accept that that is how one must live from now on: in a state of shame. Perhaps shame is nothing more than the name for the way I feel all the time. The name for the way in which people live who would prefer to be dead."

Shame. Mortification. Death in life.

There was a long silence.

"Can I borrow ten rand?" said Vercueil. "My disability comes through on Thursday. I'll pay you back then."

three

In the small hours of last night there was a telephone call. A woman, breathless, with the breathlessness of fat people. "I want to speak to Florence."

"She is sleeping. Everyone is sleeping."

"Yes, you can call her."

It was raining, though not hard. I knocked at Florence's door. At once it opened, as if she had been standing there waiting for the summons. From behind her came the sleepy groan of a child. "Telephone," I said.

Five minutes later she came up to my room. Without her

glasses, bareheaded, in a long white nightdress, she seemed much younger.

"There is trouble," she said.

"Is it Bheki?"

"Yes, I must go."

"Where is he?"

"First I must go to Guguletu, then after that, I think, to Site C."

"I have no idea where Site C is."

She gave me a puzzled look.

"I mean, if you can show me the way I will take you by car," I said.

"Yes," she said, but still hesitated. "But I cannot leave the children alone."

"Then they must come along."

"Yes," she said. I could not remember ever seeing her so indecisive.

"And Mr. Vercueil," I said. "He must come to help with the car."

She shook her head.

"Yes," I insisted. "He must come."

The dog lay at Vercueil's side. It tapped its tail on the floor when I came in but did not get up.

"Mr. Vercueil!" I said loudly. He opened his eyes; I held the light away. He broke wind. "I have to take Florence to Guguletu. It is urgent, we have to leave at once. Will you come along?"

He made no reply, but curled up on his side. The dog rearranged itself.

"Mr. Vercueil!" I said, pointing the light at him.

"Fuck off," he mumbled.

"I can't wake him," I reported to Florence. "I have to have someone along to push the car."

"I will push," she said.

With the two children on the back seat warmly covered, Florence pushed. We set off. Peering through glass misted over with our breathing, I crawled over De Waal Drive, got lost for a while in the streets of Claremont, then found Lansdowne Road. The first buses of the day were abroad, brightly lit and empty. It was not yet five o'clock.

We passed the last houses, the last streetlights. Into a steady rain from the northwest we drove, following the faint yellow glow of our headlights.

"If people wave to you to stop, or if you see things in the road, you must not stop, you must drive on," said Florence.

"I will certainly not," I said. "You should have warned me earlier. Let me make myself clear, Florence: at the first sign of trouble I am turning back."

"I do not say it will happen, I am just telling you."

Full of misgiving I drove on into the darkness. But no one barred the way, no one waved, there was nothing across the road. Trouble, it seemed, was still in bed; trouble was recuperating for the next engagement. The roadside, along which, at this hour, thousands of men would ordinarily have been plodding to work, was empty. Swirls of mist floated toward us, embraced the car, floated away. Wraiths, spirits. Aornos this place: birdless. I shivered, met Florence's gaze. "How much further?" I asked.

"Not far."

"What did they say on the telephone?"

"They were shooting again yesterday. They were giving guns to the *witdoeke* and the *witdoeke* were shooting."

"Are they shooting in Guguletu?"

"No, they are shooting out in the bush."

"At the first hint of trouble, Florence, I am turning back. We are fetching Bheki, that is all we are going to do, then we are going home. You should never have let him leave."

"Yes, but you must turn here, you must turn left."

I turned. A hundred meters further there was a barrier across the road with flashing lights, cars parked along the verges, police with guns. I stopped; a policeman came up.

"What is your business here?" he asked.

"I am taking my domestic home," I said, surprised at how calmly I lied.

He peered at the children sleeping on the back seat. "Where does she live?"

"Fifty-seven," said Florence.

"You can drop her here, she can walk, it is not far."

"It is raining, she has small children, I am not letting her walk alone," I said firmly.

He hesitated, then with his flashlight waved me through. On the roof of one of the cars stood a young man in battle dress, his gun at the ready, staring out into the darkness.

Now there was a smell of burning in the air, of wet ash, burning rubber. Slowly we drove down a broad unpaved street lined with matchbox houses. A police van armored in wire mesh cruised past us. "Turn right here," said Florence. "Turn right again. Stop here."

With the baby on her arm and the little girl, only half awake, stumbling behind, she splashed up the path to No. 219, knocked, was admitted. Hope and Beauty. It was like living in an allegory. Keeping the engine running, I waited.

The police van that had passed us drew up alongside. A light shone in my face. I held up a hand to shield my eyes. The van pulled away.

Florence reemerged holding a plastic raincoat over herself and the baby, and got into the back seat. Dashing through the rain behind her came not Bheki but a man in his thirties or forties, slight, dapper, with a mustache. He got in beside me. "This is Mr. Thabane, my cousin," said Florence. "He will show us the way."

"Where is Hope?" I asked.

"I have left her with my sister."

"And where is Bheki?"

There was silence.

"I am not sure," said the man. His voice was surprisingly soft. "He came in yesterday morning and put his things down and went out. After that we did not see him at all. He did not come home to sleep. But I know where his friends live. We can start looking there."

"Is this what you want, Florence?" I asked.

"We must look for him," said Florence. "There is nothing else we can do."

"If you would prefer me to drive I can drive," said the man. "It is anyhow better, you know."

I got out and sat beside Florence in the back. The rain was coming down more heavily now; the car splashed through pools on the uneven road. Left and right we turned under the sick orange of the streetlights, then stopped. "Careful, don't switch off," I said to Mr. Thabane the cousin.

He got out and knocked at a window. A long conversation followed with someone I could not see. By the time he came back he was soaked and cold. With clumsy fingers he took out a pack of cigarettes and tried to light one. "Please, not in the car," I said. A look of exasperation passed between him and Florence.

We sat in silence. "What are we waiting for?" I asked.

"They are sending someone to show us the way."

A little boy wearing a balaclava cap too large for him came trotting out of the house. With entire self-assurance, greeting us all with a smile, he got into the car and began to give directions. Ten years old at most. A child of the times, at home in this landscape of violence. When I think back to my own childhood I remember only long sun-struck afternoons, the smell of dust under avenues of eucalyptus, the quiet rustle of water in roadside furrows, the lulling of doves. A childhood of sleep, prelude to what was meant to be a life without trouble and a smooth passage to Nirvana. Will we at least be allowed our Nirvana, we children of that bygone age? I doubt it. If justice reigns at all, we will find ourselves barred at the first threshold of the underworld. White as grubs in our swaddling bands, we will be dispatched to join those infant souls whose eternal whining Aeneas mistook for weeping. White our color, the color of limbo: white sands, white rocks, a white light pouring down from all sides. Like an eternity of lying on the beach, an endless Sunday among thousands of our own kind, sluggish, half asleep, in earshot of the comfortable lap of the waves. *In limine primo:* on the threshold of death, the threshold of life. Creatures thrown up by the sea, stalled on the sands, undecided, indecisive, neither hot nor cold, neither fish nor fowl.

We had passed the last of the houses and were driving in gray early-morning light through a landscape of scorched earth, blackened trees. A pickup truck passed us with three men in the back sheltering under a tarpaulin. At the next road block we caught up with them again. They gazed expressionlessly at us, eye to eye, as we waited to be inspected. A policeman waved them through, waved us through too.

We turned north, away from the mountain, then off the highway onto a dirt road that soon became sand. Mr. Thabane stopped. "We can't drive further, it is too dangerous," he said. "There is something wrong with your alternator," he added, pointing to the red light glowing on the dashboard.

"I am letting things run down," I said. I did not feel like explaining.

He switched off the engine. For a while we sat listening to the rain drumming on the roof. Then Florence got out, and the boy. Tied on her back, the baby slept peacefully.

"It is best if you keep the doors locked," said Mr. Thabane to me.

"How long will you be?"

"I cannot say, but we will hurry."

I shook my head. "I am not staying here," I said.

I had no hat, no umbrella. The rain beat against my face, pasted my hair to my scalp, ran down my neck. From this sort of outing, I thought, one catches one's death of cold. The boy, our guide, had already dashed ahead.

"Put this over your head," said Mr. Thabane, offering the plastic raincoat.

"Nonsense," I said, "I don't mind a little rain."

"Still, hold it over you," he insisted. I understood. "Come," he said. I followed.

Around us was a wilderness of gray dune sand and Port Jackson willow, and a stench of garbage and ash. Shreds of plastic, old iron, glass, animal bones littered both sides of the path. I was already shivering with cold, but when I tried to walk faster my heart pounded unpleasantly. I was falling behind. Would Florence pause? No: *amor matris,* a force that stopped for nothing.

At a fork in the path Mr. Thabane was waiting. "Thank you," I gasped, "you are kind. I am sorry to be holding you up. I have a bad hip."

"Take my arm," he said.

Men passed us, dark, bearded, stern, armed with sticks, walking swiftly in single file. Mr. Thabane stepped off the path. I held tighter to him.

The path widened, then came to an end in a wide, flat pond. On the far side of the pond the shanties started, the lowest-lying cluster surrounded by water, flooded. Some built sturdily of wood and iron, others no more than skins of plastic sheeting over frames of branches, they straggled north over the dunes as far as I could see.

At the brink of the pond I hesitated. "Come," said Mr. Thabane. Holding on to him I stepped in, and we waded across, in water up to our ankles. One of my shoes was sucked off. "Watch out for broken glass," he warned. I retrieved the shoe.

Save for an old woman with a sagging mouth standing in a doorway, there was no one in sight. But as we walked further the noise we had heard, which at first might have been taken for wind and rain, began to break up into shouts, cries, calls, over a ground bass that I can only call a sigh: a deep sigh, repeated over and over, as if the wide world itself were sighing.

Then the little boy, our guide, was with us again, tugging Mr. Thabane's sleeve, talking excitedly. The two of them broke away; I struggled behind them up the duneside.

We were at the rear of a crowd hundreds strong looking down upon a scene of devastation: shanties burnt and smoldering, shanties still burning, pouring forth black smoke. Jumbles of furniture, bedding, household objects stood in the pouring rain. Gangs of men were at work trying to rescue the contents of the burning shacks, going from one to another, putting out the fires; or so I thought till with a shock it came to me that these were no rescuers but incendiaries, that the battle I saw them waging was not with the flames but with the rain.

It was from the people gathered on the rim of this amphitheater in the dunes that the sighing came. Like mourners at a funeral they stood in the downpour, men, women, and children, sodden, hardly bothering to protect themselves, watching the destruction.

A man in a black overcoat swung an ax. With a crash a window burst. He attacked the door, which caved in at the third blow. As if released from a cage, a woman with a baby in her arms flew out of the house, followed by three barefoot children. He let them pass. Then he began to hack at the doorframe. The whole structure creaked.

One of his fellows stepped inside carrying a jerry can. The woman dashed in after him, emerged with her arms full of bedclothes. But when she tried to make a second foray she was hurled out bodily.

A new sigh rose from the crowd. Wisps of smoke began to blow from inside the shack. The woman got to her feet, dashed indoors, was again hurled out.

A stone came sailing out of the crowd and fell with a clatter on the roof of the burning shack. Another hit the wall, another landed at the feet of the man with the ax. He gave a menacing shout. He and half a dozen of his fellows stopped what they were doing and, brandishing sticks and bars, advanced on the crowd. Screaming, people turned to flee, I among them. But in the clinging sand I could barely lift my feet. My heart pounded, pains shot through my chest. I stopped, bent over, gasping. *Can this really be happening to me?* I thought. *What am I doing here?* I had a vision of the little green car waiting quietly at the roadside. There was nothing I longed for more than to get into my car, slam the door behind me, close out this looming world of rage and violence.

A girl, an enormously fat teenager, shouldered me out of her way. "Damn you!" I gasped as I fell. "Damn you!" she gasped back, glaring with naked animosity. "Get out! Get out!" And she toiled up the duneside, her huge backside quaking.

One more such blow, I thought, face down in the sand, and I am gone. These people can take many blows, but I, I am fragile as a butterfly.

Feet crunched past me. I caught a glimpse of a brown boot, the tongue flapping, the sole tied on with string. The blow I shrank from did not fall.

I got up. There was a fight of some kind going on to my left; all the people who a minute ago had been fleeing into the bush were just as suddenly pouring back. A woman screamed, high and loud. How could I get away from this terrible place? Where was the pond I had waded across, where was the path to the car? There were ponds everywhere, pools, lakes, sheets of water; there were paths everywhere, but where did they lead?

Distinctly I heard the pop of gunfire, one, two, three shots, not nearby, but not far away either.

"Come," said a voice, and Mr. Thabane strode past. "Yes!"

I gasped, and gratefully struggled after him. But I could not catch up. "Slower, please," I called. He waited; together he and I recrossed the pool and reached the path.

A young man came up beside us, his eyes bloodshot. "Where are you going?" he demanded. A hard question, a hard voice.

"I am going away, I am getting away, I am out of place here," I answered.

"We are going to fetch the car," said Mr. Thabane.

"We want to use that car," said the young man.

"I am not letting anyone have my car," I said.

"This is a friend of Bheki," said Mr. Thabane.

"I don't care, I am not letting him have my car."

The young man—not a man at all, in fact, but a boy dressed like a man, bearing himself like a man—made a strange gesture: holding one hand at head height, he struck it with the other, palm against palm, a glancing blow. What did it mean? Did it mean anything?

My back was in agony from the walking. I slowed down and stopped. "I must get home soon," I said. It was an appeal; I could hear the unsteadiness in my voice.

"You have seen enough?" said Mr. Thabane, sounding more distant than before.

"Yes, I have seen enough. I didn't come here to see sights. I came to fetch Bheki."

"And you want to go home?"

"Yes, I want to go home. I am in pain, I am exhausted."

He turned and walked on. I hobbled behind. Then he stopped again. "You want to go home," he said. "But what of the people who live here? When they want to go home, this is where they must go. What do you think of that?"

We stood in the rain, in the middle of the path, face to face. Passersby stopped too, regarding me curiously, my business their business, everyone's business.

"I have no answer," I said. "It is terrible."

"It is not just terrible," he said, "it is a crime. When you see a crime being committed in front of your eyes, what do you say? Do you say, 'I have seen enough, I didn't come to see sights, I want to go home'?"

I shook my head in distress.

"No, you don't," he said. "Correct. Then what do you say? What sort of crime is it that you see? What is its name?"

He is a teacher, I thought: that is why he speaks so well. What he is doing to me he has practiced in the classroom. It is the trick one uses to make one's own answer seem to come from the child. Ventriloquism, the legacy of Socrates, as oppressive in Africa as it was in Athens.

I glanced around the ring of spectators. Were they hostile? There was no hostility I could detect. They were merely waiting for me to say my part.

"There are many things I am sure I could say, Mr. Thabane," I said. "But then they must truly come from me. When one speaks under duress—you should know this—one rarely speaks the truth."

He was going to respond, but I stopped him.

"Wait. Give me a minute. I am not evading your question. There are terrible things going on here. But what I think of them I must say in my own way."

"Then let us hear what you have to say! We are listening! We are waiting!" He raised his hands for silence. The crowd murmured approval.

"These are terrible sights," I repeated, faltering. "They are to be condemned. But I cannot denounce them in other people's words. I must find my own words, from myself. Otherwise it is not the truth. That is all I can say now."

"This woman talks shit," said a man in the crowd. He looked around. "Shit," he said. No one contradicted him. Already some were drifting away.

"Yes," I said, speaking directly to him. "You are right, what you say is true."

He gave me a look as if I were mad.

"But what do you expect?" I went on. "To speak of this"—I waved a hand over the bush, the smoke, the filth littering the path—"you would need the tongue of a god."

"Shit," he said again, challenging me.

Mr. Thabane turned and walked off. I trailed behind him. The crowd parted. In a minute the boy passed me, hurrying. Then the car came in sight.

"It is a Hillman, your car, isn't it," said Mr. Thabane. "There can't be many left on the roads."

I was surprised. After what had passed I thought there was a line drawn between us. But he seemed to bear no grudge.

"From the time when British was Best," I replied. "I am sorry if I do not make sense."

He ignored the apology, if that is what it was. "Was British ever best?" he asked.

"No, of course not. It was just a slogan for a while after the war. You won't remember, you were too young."

"I was born in 1943," he said. "I'm forty-three. Don't you believe me?" He turned, offering me his neat good looks. Vain; but an appealing vanity.

I pulled the starter. The battery was dead. Mr. Thabane and the boy got out and pushed, struggling for a footing in the sand. At last the engine caught. "Go straight," said the boy. I obeyed.

"Are you a teacher?" I asked Mr. Thabane.

"I was a teacher. But I have left the profession temporarily. Till better times arrive. At present I sell shoes."

"And you?" I asked the boy.

He mumbled something I did not hear.

"He is an unemployed youth," said Mr. Thabane. "Are you not?"

The boy smiled self-consciously. "Turn here, just after the shops," he said.

Alone in the wilderness stood a row of three little shops, gutted, scorched. BHAWOODIEN CASH STORE, said the one sign still legible.

"From long ago," said Mr. Thabane. "From last year."

We had come out on a broad dirt road. To our left stood a cluster of houses, proper houses, with brick walls and asbestos roofs and chimneys. Among them, around them, stretching into the distance across the flats, were squatter shacks.

"That building," said the boy, pointing ahead.

It was a long, low building, a hall or school perhaps, surrounded by a mesh fence. But great lengths of the fence had been trampled down, and of the building itself only the smoke-blackened walls were still standing. In front of it a crowd had gathered. Faces turned to watch the Hillman's approach.

"Shall I switch off?" I said.

"You can switch off, there is nothing to be afraid of," said Mr. Thabane.

"I am not afraid," I said. Was it true? In a sense, yes; or at least, after the episode in the bush, I cared less what happened to me.

"There is no need to be afraid anyway," he continued smoothly. "Your boys are here to protect you." And he pointed.

I saw them then, further down the road: three khaki-brown troop carriers almost merging into the trees, and, outlined against the sky, helmeted heads.

"In case you were thinking," he concluded, "that this was just a quarrel among blacks, a spot of faction fighting. Look: there is my sister."

My sister he called her, not *Florence*. Perhaps I alone in all the world called her Florence. Called her by an alias. Now I was on ground where people were revealed in their true names.

She stood with her back to the wall, sheltering from the rain: a sober, respectable woman in a burgundy coat and white knitted cap. We threaded our way toward her. Though she gave no sign, I was sure she saw me. "Florence!" I called. She looked up dully. "Have you found him?"

She nodded toward the gutted interior, then turned away, not greeting me. Mr. Thabane began to push past the throng in the entranceway. Embarrassed, I waited. People milled past, skirting me as though I were bad luck.

A girl in an apple-green school tunic advanced on me, her hand raised as if to give me a slap. I flinched, but it was only in play. Or perhaps I should say: she forbore from actually striking.

"I think you should look too," said Mr. Thabane, reemerging, breathing fast. He went over to Florence and took her in his arms. Lifting her glasses aside, she put her head on his shoulder and burst into tears.

The inside of the hall was a mess of rubble and charred beams. Against the far wall, shielded from the worst of the rain, were five bodies neatly laid out. The body in the middle was that of Florence's Bheki. He still wore the gray flannel trousers, white shirt, and maroon pullover of his school, but his feet were bare. His eyes were open and staring, his mouth open too. The rain had been beating on him for hours, on him and his comrades, not only here but wherever they had been when they met their deaths; their clothes, their very hair, had a flattened, dead look. In the corners of his eyes there were grains of sand. There was sand in his mouth.

Someone was tugging my arm. Dazed, I looked down at a little girl with wide, solemn eyes. "Sister," she said, "sister . . . ," but then did not know how to go on.

"She is asking, are you one of the sisters," explained a woman, smiling benignly.

I did not want to be drawn away, not now. I shook my head.

"She means, are you one of the sisters from the Catholic church," said the woman. "No," she went on, speaking to the child in English, "she is not one of the sisters." Gently she unlocked the child's fingers from my sleeve.

Florence was surrounded by a press of people.

"Must they lie there in the rain?" I asked Mr. Thabane.

"Yes, they must lie there. So that everyone can see."

"But who did it?"

I was shaking: shivers ran up and down my body, my hands trembled. I thought of the boy's open eyes. I thought: What did he see as his last sight on earth? I thought: This is the worst thing I have witnessed in my life. And I thought: Now my eyes are open and I can never close them again.

"Who did it?" said Mr. Thabane. "If you want to dig the bullets out of their bodies, you are welcome. But I will tell you in advance what you will find. 'Made in South Africa. SABS Approved.' That is what you will find."

"Please listen to me," I said. "I am not indifferent to this . . . this war. How can I be? No bars are thick enough to keep it out." I felt like crying; but here, beside Florence, what right had I? "It lives inside me and I live inside it," I whispered.

Mr. Thabane shrugged impatiently. His look had grown uglier. No doubt I grow uglier too by the day. Metamorphosis, that thickens our speech, dulls our feelings, turns us into beasts. Where on these shores does the herb grow that will preserve us from it?

I tell you the story of this morning mindful that the storyteller, from her office, claims the place of right. It is through my eyes that you see; the voice that speaks in your head is mine. Through me alone do you find yourself here on these desolate flats, smell the smoke in the air, see the bodies of the dead, hear the weeping, shiver in the rain. It is my thoughts that you think, my despair that you feel, and also the first stirrings of welcome for whatever will put an end to thought: sleep, death. To me your sympathies flow; your heart beats with mine.

Now, my child, flesh of my flesh, my best self, I ask you to draw back. I tell you this story not so that you will feel for me but so that you will learn how things are. It would be easier for you, I know, if the story came from someone else, if it were a stranger's voice sounding in your ear. But the fact is, there is no one else. I am the only one. I am the one writing:

I, I. So I ask you: attend to the writing, not to me. If lies and pleas and excuses weave among the words, listen for them. Do not pass them over, do not forgive them easily. Read all, even this adjuration, with a cold eye.

Someone had thrown a rock through the windscreen. Big as a child's head, mute, it lay on the seat amid a scattering of glass as if it now owned the car. My first thought was: Where will I get a windscreen for a Hillman? And then: How fortunate that everything is coming to an end at the same time!

I tumbled the rock from the seat and began to pick out the loose shards from the windscreen. Now that I had something to do I felt calmer. But I was calmer too because I no longer cared if I lived. What might happen to me no longer mattered. I thought: My life may as well be waste. We shoot these people as if they are waste, but in the end it is we whose lives are not worth living.

I thought of the five bodies, of their massive, solid presence in the burned-down hall. Their ghosts have not departed, I thought, and will not depart. Their ghosts are sitting tight, in possession.

If someone had dug a grave for me there and then in the sand, and pointed, I would without a word have climbed in and lain down and folded my hands on my breast. And when the sand fell in my mouth and in the corners of my eyes I would not have lifted a finger to brush it away.

Do not read in sympathy with me. Let your heart not beat with mine.

I held out a coin through the window. There was a rush of takers. The children pushed, the engine started. Into thrust-out hands I emptied my purse.

Drawn up among the bushes where the road dwindled to a track stood the military vehicles I had seen, not three, as I had thought, but five. Under the eye of a boy in an olive rain cape I got out of the car, so cold in my wet clothes that I might as well have been naked.

I had hoped the words I needed would just come, but they did not. I held out my hands, palms upward. I am bereft, my hands said, bereft of speech. I come to speak but have nothing to say.

"Wag in die motor, ek sal die polisie skakel," he called down to me. A boy with pimples playing this self-important, murderous game. Wait in the car, I will call the police. I shook my head, went on shaking my head. He was talking to someone beside him, someone I could not see. He was smiling. No doubt they had been watching from the beginning, had their own opinion of me. A mad old do-gooder caught in the rain, bedraggled as a hen. Were they right? Am I a do-gooder? No, I have done no good that I can think of. Am I mad? Yes, I am mad. But they are mad too. All of us running mad, possessed by devils. When madness climbs the throne, who in the land escapes contagion?

"Don't call the police, I can take care of myself," I called. But the murmuring, the sideways looks, continued. Perhaps they were already on the radio.

"What do you think you are doing?" I called up to the boy. The smile stiffened on his lips. *"What do you think you are doing?"* I shouted, my voice beginning to crack. Shocked, he stared down. Shocked to be screamed at by a white woman, and one old enough to be his grandmother.

A man in battle dress came over from the next vehicle in

the line. Levelly he regarded me. *"Wat is die moeilikheid?"* he asked the boy in the troop carrier. *"Nee, niks moeilikheid nie."* No problem. *"Net hierdie dame wat wil weet wat aangaan."*

"This is a dangerous place to be, lady," he said, turning to me. An officer, evidently. "Anything can happen here. I am going to send for an escort to take you back to the road."

I shook my head. I was in command of myself, I was not even tearful, though I did not put it past myself to break down at any moment.

What did I want? What did the old lady want? What she wanted was to bare something to them, whatever there was that might be bared at this time, in this place. What she wanted, before they got rid of her, was to bring out a scar, a hurt, to force it upon them, to make them see it with their own eyes: a scar, any scar, the scar of all this suffering, but in the end my scar, since our own scars are the only scars we can carry with us. I even brought a hand up to the buttons of my dress. But my fingers were blue, frozen.

"Have you seen inside that hall?" I asked in my cracked voice. Now the tears were beginning to come.

The officer dropped his cigarette, ground it into the wet sand.

"This unit hasn't fired a shot in twenty-four hours," he said softly. "Let me suggest to you: don't get upset before you know what you are talking about. Those people in there are not the only ones who have died. The killings are going on all the time. Those are just the bodies they picked up from yesterday. The fighting has subsided for the time being, but as soon as the rain stops it will flare up again. I don't know how you got here—they should have closed the road—but this is a bad place, you shouldn't be here. We'll radio the police, they can escort you out."

"Ek het reeds geskakel," said the boy in the troop carrier.

"Why don't you just put down your guns and go home, all of you?" I said. "Because surely nothing can be worse than what you are doing here. Worse for your souls, I mean."

"No," he said. I had expected incomprehension, but no, he understood exactly what I meant. "We will see it through now."

I was shivering from head to foot. My fingers, curled into the palms of my hands, would not straighten. The wind drove the sodden clothing against my skin.

"I knew one of those dead boys," I said. "I have known him since he was five. His mother works for me. You are all too young for this. It sickens me. That is all."

I drove back to the hall and, sitting in the car, waited. They were bringing the bodies out now. From the gathering crowd I felt a wave of something come out at me: resentment, animosity. Worse than that: hatred. Would it have been different if I had not been seen speaking to the soldiers? No.

Mr. Thabane came over to see what I wanted. "I am sorry, but I am not sure of the way back," I said.

"Get onto the tar road, turn right, follow the signs," he said curtly.

"Yes, but which signs?"

"The signs to civilization." And he turned on his heel.

I drove slowly, in part because of the wind beating into my face, in part because I was numb in body and soul. I strayed into a suburb I had never heard of and spent twenty minutes driving around indistinguishable streets looking for a way out.

At last I found myself in Voortrekker Road. Here, for the first time, people began to stare at the car with the shattered windscreen. Stares followed me all the way home.

The house felt cold and alien. I told myself: Have a hot bath, rest. But an icy lethargy possessed me. It took an effort to drag myself upstairs, peel off the wet clothes, wrap myself in a robe, get into bed. Sand, the gray sand of the Cape Flats, had crusted between my toes. I will never be warm again, I thought. Vercueil has a dog to lie against. Vercueil knows how to live in this climate. But as for me, and for that cold boy soon to be put into the earth, no dog will help us anymore. Sand already in his mouth, creeping in, claiming him.

Sixteen years since I shared a bed with man or boy. Sixteen years alone. Does that surprise you?

I wrote. I write. I follow the pen, going where it takes me. What else have I now?

I woke up haggard. It was night again. Where had the day gone?

The light in the toilet was on. Sitting on the seat, his trousers around his knees, his hat on his head, fast asleep, was Vercueil. I stared in astonishment.

He did not wake; on the contrary, though his head lolled and his jaw hung open, he slept as sweetly as a babe. His long lean thigh was quite hairless.

The kitchen door stood open and garbage from the overturned bucket was strewn over the floor. Worrying at an old wrapping paper was the dog. When it saw me it hung its ears guiltily and thumped its tail. "Too much!" I murmured. "Too much!" The dog slunk out.

I sat down at the table and gave myself up to tears. I cried not for the confusion in my head, not for the mess in the house, but for the boy, for Bheki. Wherever I turned he was before me, his eyes open in the look of childish puzzlement with which he had met his death. Head on arms I sobbed, grieving for him, for what had been taken from him, for what had been taken from me. Such a good thing, life! Such a wonderful idea for God to have had! The best idea there had ever been. A gift, the most generous of all gifts, renewing itself endlessly through the generations. And now Bheki, robbed of it, gone, torn away!

"I want to go home!" So I had whinged, to my shame, to Mr. Thabane the shoe salesman. From an old person's throat a child's voice. Home to my safe house, to my bed of childhood slumber. Have I ever been fully awake? I might as well ask: Do the dead know they are dead? No: to the dead it is not given to know anything. But in our dead sleep we may at least be visited by intimations. I have intimations older than any memory, unshakable, that once upon a time I was alive. Was alive and then was stolen from life. From the cradle a theft took place: a child was taken and a doll left in its place to be nursed and reared, and that doll is what I call I.

A doll? A doll's life? Is that what I have lived? Is it given to a doll to conceive such a thought? Or does the thought come and go as another intimation, a flash of lightning, a piercing of the fog by the lance of an angel's intelligence? Can a doll recognize a doll? Can a doll know death? No: dolls grow, they acquire speech and gait, they perambulate the world; they age, they wither, they perish; they are wheeled into the fire or buried in the earth; but they do not die. They exist forever in that moment of petrified surprise prior to all recollection when a life was taken away, a life not theirs but in whose place they are left behind as a token. Their knowing a knowledge without substance, without worldly weight, like a doll's head itself, empty, airy. As they themselves are not babies but the ideas of babies, more round, more pink, more blank and blue-eyed than a baby could ever be, living not life but an idea of life, immortal, undying, like all ideas.

Hades, Hell: the domain of ideas. Why has it ever been necessary that hell be a place on its own in the ice of Antarctica or down the pit of a volcano? Why can hell not be at the foot of Africa, and why can the creatures of hell not walk among the living?

"Father, can't you see I'm burning?" implored the child, standing at his father's bedside. But his father, sleeping on, dreaming, did not see.

That is the reason—I bring it forward now for you to see—why I cling so tightly to the memory of my mother. For if she did not give me life, no one did. I cling not just to the memory of her but to her herself, to her body, to my birth from her body into the world. In blood and milk I drank her body and came to life. And then was stolen, and have been lost ever since.

There is a photograph of me you have seen but will probably not remember. It was taken in 1918, when I was not yet two. I am on my feet; I appear to be reaching toward the camera; my mother, kneeling behind me, restrains me by some kind of rein that passes over my shoulders. Standing to one side, ignoring me, is my brother, Paul, his cap at a jaunty angle.

My brow is furrowed, my eyes are fixed intensely on the camera. Am I merely squinting into the sun or, like the savages of Borneo, do I have a shadowy sense that the camera will rob me of my soul? Worse: does my mother hold me back from striking the camera to the ground because I, in my doll's way, know that it will see what the eye cannot: that I am not there? And does my mother know this because she too is not there?

Paul, dead, to whom the pen has led me. I held his hand when he was going. I whispered to him, "You will see Mama, you will both be so happy." He was pale, even his eyes had the blanched hue of far-off sky. He gave me a tired, empty look as if to say: How little you understand! Did Paul ever really live? My sister life, he called me once in a letter, in borrowed words. Did it come to him at the end that he had made a mistake? Did those translucent eyes see through me?

We were photographed, that day, in a garden. There are flowers behind us that look like hollyhocks; to our left is a bed of melons. I recognize the place. It is Uniondale, the house in Church Street bought by my grandfather when ostrich feathers were booming. Year after year fruit and flowers and vegetables burgeoned in that garden, pouring forth their seed, dying, resurrecting themselves, blessing us with their profuse presence. But by whose love tended? Who clipped the hollyhocks? Who laid the melon seeds in their warm, moist bed? Was it my grandfather who got up at four in the icy morning to open the sluice and lead water into the garden? If not he, then whose was the garden rightfully? Who are the ghosts and who the presences? Who, outside the picture, leaning on their rakes, leaning on their spades, waiting to get back to work, lean also against the edge of the rectangle, bending it, bursting it in?

Dies irae, dies illa when the absent shall be present and the present absent. No longer does the picture show who were in the garden frame that day, but who were not there. Lying all these years in places of safekeeping across the country, in albums, in desk drawers, this picture and thousands like it have subtly matured, metamorphosed. The fixing did not hold or the developing went further than one would ever have dreamed—who can know how it happened?—but they have become negatives again, a new kind of negative in which we begin to see what used to lie outside the frame, occulted.

Is that why my brow is furrowed, is that why I struggle to reach the camera: do I obscurely know that the camera is the enemy, that the camera will not lie about us but uncover what we truly are: doll-folk? Am I struggling against the reins in order to strike the camera out of the hands of whoever holds it before it is too late? And who holds the camera? Whose formless shadow leans toward my mother and her two off-spring across the tilled bed?

Grief past weeping. I am hollow, I am a shell. To each of us fate sends the right disease. Mine a disease that eats me out from inside. Were I to be opened up they would find me hollow as a doll, a doll with a crab sitting inside licking its lips, dazed by the flood of light.

Was it the crab I saw so presciently when I was two, peeping out of the black box? Was I trying to save us all from the crab? But they held me back, they pressed the button, and the crab sprang out and entered me.

Gnawing at my bones now that there is no flesh left. Gnawing the socket of my hip, gnawing my backbone, beginning to gnaw at my knees. The cats, if the truth be told, have never really loved me. Only this creature is faithful to the end. My pet, my pain.

I went upstairs and opened the toilet door. Vercueil was still there, slumped in his deep sleep. I shook him. "Mr. Vercueil!" I said. One eye opened. "Come and lie down."

But he did not. First I heard him on the stairs, taking one step at a time like an old man. Then I heard the back door close.

A beautiful day, one of those still winter days when light seems to stream evenly from all quarters of the sky. Vercueil drove me down Breda Street and into Orange Street. Across from Government Avenue I told him to park.

"I thought of driving the car all the way down the Avenue," I said. "Once I am past the chain, I don't see how anyone can stop me. But do you think there is room to get past?"

(You may remember, there are two cast-iron bollards at the head of the Avenue with a chain stretched between them.)

"Yes, you can get past at the side," he said.

"After that it would just be a matter of keeping the car straight."

"Are you really going to do this?" he asked. His chicken-eyes glinted cruelly.

"If I can find the courage."

"But why? What for?"

Hard to make grand responses in the teeth of that look. I closed my eyes and tried to hold on to my vision of the car, moving fast enough for the flames to fan out backward, rolling down the paved avenue past the tourists and tramps and lovers, past the museum, the art gallery, the botanical gardens, till it slowed down and came to rest before the house of shame, burning and melting.

"We can go back now," I said. "I just wanted to make sure it could be done."

He came indoors and I gave him tea. The dog sat at his feet, cocking its ears at us in turn as we spoke. A nice dog: a bright presence, star-born, as some people are.

"To answer your question 'What for?' " I said: "it has to do with my life. To do with a life that isn't worth much anymore. I am trying to work out what I can get for it."

His hand moved restfully over the dog's fur, back and forth. The dog blinked, closed its eyes. Love, I thought: however unlikely, it is love I witness here.

I tried again. "There is a famous novel in which a woman is convicted of adultery—adultery was a crime in the old days—and condemned to go in public with the letter *A* stitched on her dress. She wears the *A* for so many years that people forget what it stands for. They forget that it stands for anything. It simply becomes something she wears, like a ring or a brooch. It may even be that she was the one to start the fashion of wearing writing on one's clothing. But that isn't in the book.

"These public shows, these manifestations—this is the point of the story—how can one ever be sure what they stand for? An old woman sets herself on fire, for instance. Why? Because she has been driven mad? Because she is in despair? Because she has cancer? I thought of painting a letter on the car to explain. But what? *A? B? C?* What is the right letter for my case? And why explain anyway? Whose business is it but my own?"

I might have said more, but at that moment the gate latch clicked and the dog began to growl. Two women, one of whom I recognized as Florence's sister, came up the path carrying suitcases.

"Good afternoon," said the sister. She held up a key. "We have come to fetch my sister's things. Florence."

"Yes," I said.

They let themselves into Florence's room. After a while I followed. "Is Florence all right?" I asked.

The sister, who had been unpacking a drawer, stood up straight, breathing heavily. Clearly she relished this foolish question.

"No, I cannot say she is all right," she said. "Not *all right*. How can she be *all right*?"

The other woman, pretending not to hear, continued to fold baby clothes. There was far more in the room than they could carry in two suitcases.

"I didn't mean that," I said, "but never mind. Can I ask you to take something to Florence from me?"

"Yes, I can take it if it is not big."

I wrote out a check.

"Tell Florence I am sorry. Tell her I am more sorry than I can say. I think of Bheki all the time."

"You are sorry."

"Yes."

Another day of clear skies. Vercueil in a strangely excited state. "So today is the day?" he asked. "Yes," I replied, stiffening against his indecent eagerness, on the point of adding: "But what business is it of yours?"

Yes, I said: today is the day. Yet today has passed and I have not gone through with what I promised. For as long as the trail of words continues, you know with certainty that I have not gone through with it: a rule, another rule. Death may indeed be the last great foe of writing, but writing is also the foe of death. Therefore, writing, holding death at arm's length, let me tell you that I meant to go through with it, began to go through with it, did not go through with it. Let me tell you more. Let me tell you that I bathed. Let me tell you that I dressed. Let me tell you that, as I prepared my body, some faint glow of pride began to return to it. Between waiting in bed for the breathing to stop and going out to make one's own end, what a difference!

I meant to go through with it: is that the truth? Yes. No. Yes-no. There is such a word, but it has never been allowed into the dictionaries. Yes-no: every woman knows what it means as it defeats every man. "Are you going to do it?" asked Vercueil, his man-eyes gleaming. "Yes-no," I should have answered.

I wore white and blue: a light-blue suit, a white blouse with a bow at the throat. I did my face carefully, and my hair. All the while I sat in front of the mirror I was trembling lightly. I felt no pain at all. The crab had stopped gnawing.

Luminous with curiosity, Vercueil followed me into the kitchen and prowled about while I was having breakfast. At last, irritated, unsettled, I burst out: "Would you please leave me alone!" At which he turned away with a look of such childish hurt that I gave his sleeve a tug. "I didn't mean that," I said. "But please sit down: you make me nervous when I need calm. I veer back and forth so much! At one moment I think: Let me hurry to put an end to it, to this worthless life. At the next I think: But why should I bear the blame? Why should I be expected to rise above my times? Is it my doing that my times have been so shameful? Why should it be left to me, old and sick and full of pain, to lift myself unaided out of this pit of disgrace?

"I want to rage against the men who have created these times. I want to accuse them of spoiling my life in the way that a rat or a cockroach spoils food without even eating it, simply by walking over it and sniffing it and performing its bodily functions on it. It is childish, I know, to point fingers and blame others. But why should I accept that my life would have been worthless no matter who held power in this land? Power is power, after all. It invades. That is its nature. It invades one's life.

"You want to know what is going on with me and I am trying to tell you. I want to sell myself, redeem myself, but am full of confusion about how to do it. That, if you like, is the craziness that has got into me. You need not be surprised. You know this country. There is madness in the air here."

Throughout this speech Vercueil had worn the same tight, secretive little look. Now he said a strange thing: "Would you like to go for a drive?"

"We can't go for a drive, Mr. Vercueil. There are a thousand reasons why we can't."

"We can see some sights, be back by twelve o'clock."

"We can't go sightseeing in a car with a hole in the windscreen. It is ridiculous."

"I'll take out the windscreen. It's just glass, you don't need it."

Why did I give in? Perhaps what won me in the end was the new attention he was paying me. He was like a boy in a state of excitement, sexual excitement, and I was his object. I was flattered; in a distant way, despite all, I was even amused.

Obscurely I may have felt something unsavory in it, as in the excitement of a dog digging for carrion not buried deep enough. But I was in no condition to draw lines. What did I want, after all? I wanted a suspension. To be suspended without thought, without pain, without doubt, without apprehension, till noon came. Till the noonday gun boomed on Signal Hill and, with a bottle of petrol on the seat beside me, I either drove or did not drive past the chain and down the Avenue. But to be thoughtless till then; to hear birds sing, to feel the air on my skin, to see the sky. To live.

So I yielded. Vercueil wrapped a towel around his hand and broke out more of the glass till the hole was big enough for a child to climb through. I gave him the key. A push, and we were away.

Like lovers revisiting the scenes of their first declarations, we took the mountainside drive above Muizenberg. (Lovers! What had I ever declared to Vercueil? That he should stop drinking. What had he declared to me? Nothing: perhaps not even his true name.) We parked at the same spot as before. Now: feast a last time on these sights, I told myself, digging my nails into my palms, staring out over False Bay, bay of false hope, and southward over the bleak winter waters of the most neglected of oceans.

"If we had a boat you could take me out to sea," I murmured.

Southward: Vercueil and I alone, sailing till we reached the latitudes where albatrosses fly. Where he could lash me to a barrel or a plank, it did not matter which, and leave me bobbing on the waves under the great white wings.

Vercueil reversed onto the road. Was I wrong, or did the engine throb more sweetly in his hands than in mine?

"I am sorry if I am not making sense," I said. "I am trying my best not to lose direction. I am trying to keep up a sense of urgency. A sense of urgency is what keeps deserting me. Sitting here among all this beauty, or even sitting at home among my own things, it seems hardly possible to believe there is a zone of killing and degradation all around me. It seems like a bad dream. Something presses, nudges inside me. I try to take no notice, but it insists. I yield an inch; it presses harder. With relief I give in, and life is suddenly ordinary again. With relief I give myself back to the ordinary. I wallow in it. I lose my sense of shame, become shameless as a child. The shamefulness of that shamelessness: that is what I cannot forget, that is what I cannot bear afterward. That is why I must take hold of myself, point myself down the path. Otherwise I am lost. Do you understand?"

Vercueil crouched over the wheel like someone with poor eyesight. He of the hawk's-eye. Did it matter if he did not understand?

"It is like trying to give up alcohol," I persisted. "Trying and trying, always trying, but knowing in your bones from the beginning that you are going to slide back. There is a shame to that private knowledge, a shame so warm, so intimate, so comforting that it brings more shame flooding with it. There seems to be no limit to the shame a human being can feel.

"But how hard it is to kill oneself! One clings so tight to life! It seems to me that something other than the will must come into play at the last instant, something foreign, something thoughtless, to sweep you over the brink. You have to become someone other than yourself. But who? Who is it that waits for me to step into his shadow? Where do I find him?"

My watch said 10:20. "We have to go back," I said.

Vercueil slowed down. "If that is what you want, I'll take you back," he said. "Or, if you like, we can go on driving. We can drive all the way round the Peninsula. It's a nice day."

I should have answered: No, take me back at once. But I hesitated, and in that moment of hesitation the words died within me.

"Stop here," I said.

Vercueil drew off the road and parked.

"I have a favor to ask of you," I said. "Please don't make fun of me."

"Is that the favor?"

"Yes. Now or in the future."

He shrugged.

On the far side of the road a man in tattered clothes sat beside a pyramid of firewood for sale. He looked us over, looked away.

Time passed.

"I told you a story once about my mother," I said at last, trying to speak more softly. "About how when she was a little girl she lay in the dark not knowing what was rolling over her, the wagon wheels or the stars.

"I have held on to that story all my life. If each of us has a story we tell to ourself about who we are and where we come from, then that is my story. That is the story I choose, or the story that has chosen me. It is there that I come from, it is there that I begin.

"You ask whether I want to go on driving. If it were practically possible, I would suggest that we drive to the Eastern Cape, to the Outeniqua Mountains, to that stopping place at the top of Prince Alfred's Pass. I would even say,

Leave maps behind, drive north and east by the sun, I will recognize it when we come to it: the stopping place, the starting place, the place of the navel, the place where I join the world. Drop me off there, at the top of the pass, and drive away, leaving me to wait for the night and the stars and the ghostly wagon to come rolling over.

"But the truth is, with or without maps, I can no longer find the place. Why? Because a certain desire has gone from me. A year ago or a month ago it would have been different. A desire, perhaps the deepest desire I am capable of, would have flowed from me toward that one spot of earth, guiding me. *This is my mother,* I would have said, kneeling there. *This is what gives life to me.* Holy ground, not as a grave but as a place of resurrection is holy: resurrection eternal out of the earth.

"Now that desire, which one may as well call love, is gone from me. I do not love this land anymore. It is as simple as that. I am like a man who has been castrated. Castrated in maturity. I try to imagine how life is for a man to whom that has been done. I imagine him seeing things he has loved before, knowing from memory that he ought still to love them, but able no longer to summon up the love itself. Love: what was that? he would say to himself, groping in memory for the old feeling. But about everything there would now be a flatness, a stillness, a calmness. Something I once had has been betrayed, he would think, and concentrate, trying to feel that betrayal in all its keenness. But there would be no keenness. Keenness would be what would be gone from everything. Instead he would feel a tug, light but continual, toward stupor, detachment. *Detached,* he would say to himself, pronouncing the sharp word, and he would reach out to test its sharpness. But there too a blurring, a blunting would have intervened. All is receding, he would think; in a week, in a month I will have forgotten everything, I will be among the lotus eaters, separated, drifting. For a last time he would try to feel the pain of that separation, but all that would come to him would be a fleeting sadness.

"I don't know whether I am being plain enough, Mr. Vercueil. I am talking about resolve, about trying to hold on to my resolve and failing. I confess, I am drowning. I am sitting here next to you and drowning."

Vercueil slouched against the door. The dog whined softly. Standing with its paws on the front seat, it peered ahead, eager to get moving again. A minute passed.

Then from his jacket pocket he drew a box of matches and held it out to me. "Do it now," he said.

"Do what?"

"It."

"Is that what you want?"

"Do it now. I'll get out of the car. Do it, here, now."

At the corner of his mouth a ball of spittle danced up and down. Let him be mad, I thought. Let it be possible to say that about him: that he is cruel, mad, a mad dog.

He shook the box of matches at me. "Are you worried about him?" He gestured at the man with the firewood. "He won't interfere."

"Not here," I said.

"We can go to Chapman's Peak. You can drive over the edge if that's what you want."

It was like being trapped in a car with a man trying to seduce you and getting cross when you did not give in. It was like being transported back to the worst days of girlhood.

"Can we go home?" I said.

"I thought you wanted to do it."

"You don't understand."

"I thought you wanted a push down the path. I'm giving you a push."

Outside the hotel in Hout Bay he stopped the car again. "Have you got some money for me?" he said.

I gave him a ten-rand note.

He went into the off-license, returned with a bottle in a brown paper packet. "Have a drink," he said, and twisted off the cap.

"No, thank you. I don't like brandy."

"It's not brandy, it's medicine."

I took a sip, tried to swallow, choked, and coughed; my teeth came loose.

"Hold it in your mouth," he said.

I took another sip and held it in my mouth. My gums and palate burned, then grew dead. I swallowed and closed my eyes. Something began to lift inside me: a curtain, a cloud. Is this it, then? I thought. Is this all? Is this how Vercueil points the way?

He turned the car, drove back up the hill, and parked in a picnic area high above the bay. He drank and offered me the bottle. Cautiously I drank. The veil of grayness that had covered everything grew visibly lighter. Dubious, marveling, I thought: Is it really so simple—not a matter of life and death at all?

"Let me tell you finally," I said. "What set me off was not my own condition, my sickness, but something quite different."

The dog complained softly. Vercueil reached out a languid hand; it licked his fingers.

"Florence's boy was shot on Tuesday."

He nodded.

"I saw the body," I went on, taking another sip, thinking: Shall I now grow loquacious? Lord preserve me! And as I grow loquacious will Vercueil grow loquacious too? He and I, under the influence, loquacious together in the little car?

"I was shaken," I said. "I won't say *grieved* because I have no right to the word, it belongs to his own people. But I am still—what?—disturbed. It has something to do with his deadness, his dead weight. It is as though in death he became very heavy, like lead or like that thick, airless mud you get at the bottoms of dams. As though in the act of dying he gave a last sigh and all the lightness went out of him. Now he is lying on top of me with all that weight. Not pressing, just lying.

"It was the same when that friend of his was bleeding in the street. There was the same heaviness. Heavy blood. I was trying to stop it from flowing down the gutters. So much blood! If I had caught it all I would not have been able to lift the bucket. Like trying to lift a bucket of lead.

"I have not seen black people in their death before, Mr. Vercueil. They are dying all the time, I know, but always somewhere else. The people I have seen die have been white and have died in bed, growing rather dry and light there, rather papery, rather airy. They burned well, I am sure, leaving a minimum of ash to sweep up afterward. Do you want to know why I set my mind on burning myself? Because I thought I would burn well.

"Whereas these people will not burn, Bheki and the other dead. It would be like trying to burn figures of pig iron or lead. They might lose their sharpness of contour, but when the flames subsided they would still be there, heavy as ever. Leave

them long enough and they may sink, millimeter by millimeter, till the earth closes over them. But then they would sink
no further. They would stay there, bobbing just under the
surface. If you so much as scuffled with your shoe you would
uncover them: the faces, the dead eyes, open, full of sand."

"Drink," said Vercueil, holding out the bottle. His face was
changing, the lips filling out, gorged, wet, the eyes growing
vague. Like the woman he had brought home. I took the bottle
and wiped it on my sleeve.

"You must understand, it is not just a personal thing, this
disturbance I am telling you about," I pursued. "In fact it is
not personal at all. I was fond of Bheki, certainly, when he
was still a child, but I was not happy with the way he turned
out. I had hoped for something else. He and his comrades say
they have put childhood behind them. Well, they may have
ceased being children, but what have they become? Dour little
puritans, despising laughter, despising play.

"So why should I grieve for him? The answer is, I saw his
face. When he died he was a child again. The mask must have
dropped in sheer childish surprise when it broke upon him in
that last instant that the stone-throwing and shooting was not
a game after all; that the giant who came shambling toward
him with a paw full of sand to stop into his mouth would not
be turned away by chants or slogans; that at the end of the long
passageway where he choked and gagged and could not
breathe there was no light.

"Now that child is buried and we walk upon him. Let me
tell you, when I walk upon this land, this South Africa, I have
a gathering feeling of walking upon black faces. They are dead
but their spirit has not left them. They lie there heavy and
obdurate, waiting for my feet to pass, waiting for me to go,

waiting to be raised up again. Millions of figures of pig iron floating under the skin of the earth. The age of iron waiting to return.

"You think I am upset but will get over it. Cheap tears, you think, tears of sentiment, here today, gone tomorrow. Well, it is true, I have been upset in the past, I have imagined there could be no worse, and then the worse has arrived, as it does without fail, and I have got over it, or seemed to. But that is the trouble! In order not to be paralyzed with shame I have had to live a life of getting over the worse. What I cannot get over any more is that *getting over*. If I get over it this time I will never have another chance *not* to get over it. For the sake of my own resurrection I cannot get over it this time."

Vercueil held out the bottle. A full four inches were gone. I pushed his hand away. "I don't want to drink any more," I said.

"Go on," he said. "Get drunk for a change."

"No!" I exclaimed. A tipsy anger flared up in me against his crudity, his indifference. What was I doing here? In the exhausted car the two of us must have looked like nothing so much as belated refugees from the *platteland* of the Great Depression. All we lacked was a coir mattress and a chicken coop tied on the roof. I snatched the bottle from his hand; but while I was still rolling down the window to throw it out, he wrested it back.

"Get out of my car!" I snapped.

Taking the key from the ignition lock, he got out. The dog bounded after him. In full sight of me he tossed the key into the bushes, turned, and, bottle in hand, stalked down the hill toward Hout Bay.

Burning with rage, I waited, but he did not turn.

Minutes passed. A car pulled off the road and drew up beside me. Music blared from it, loud and metallic. In that welter of noise a couple sat gazing over the sea. South Africa at its recreations. I got out and tapped at their window. The man turned a vacant look on me, chewing. "Can you turn down the music?" I said. He fiddled or pretended to fiddle with something, but the volume did not change. I tapped again. Through the glass he mouthed words at me, then in a flurry of dust reversed the car and parked on the other side of the area.

I searched in the bushes where Vercueil had thrown the key, with no success.

As the other car drove off at last, the woman turned to glare at me. Her face not unattractive yet ugly: closed, bunched, as if afraid that light, air, life itself were going to gather and strike her. Not a face but an expression, yet an expression worn so long as to be hers, her. A thickening of the membrane between the world and the self inside, a thickening become thickness. Evolution, but evolution backward. Fish from the primitive depths (I am sure you know this) grew patches of skin sensitive to the fingerings of light, patches that in time became eyes. Now, in South Africa, I see eyes clouding over again, scales thickening on them, as the land explorers, the colonists, prepare to return to the deep.

Should I have come when you invited me? In my weaker moments I have often longed to cast myself on your mercy. How lucky, for both our sakes, that I have held out! You do not need an albatross from the old world around your neck; and as for me, would I truly escape South Africa by running to you? How do I know the scales are not already thickening over my own eyes? That woman in the car: perhaps, as they drove off, she was saying to her companion: "What a sour old creature! What a closed-off face!"

And then, what honor is there in slipping off in these times when the worm-riddled ship is so clearly sinking, in the company of tennis players and crooked brokers and generals with pocketfuls of diamonds departing to set up retreats in the quieter backwaters of the world? General G., Minister M. on their holdings in Paraguay, grilling beefsteaks over coals under southern skies, drinking beer with their cronies, singing songs of the old country, looking to pass away in their sleep at a great old age with grandchildren and peons hat in hand at the foot of the bed: the Afrikaners of Paraguay joining the Afrikaners of Patagonia in their sullen diaspora: ruddy men with paunches and fat wives and gun collections on their living-room walls and safety-deposit boxes in Rosario, exchanging Sunday-afternoon visits with the sons and daughters of Barbie, Eichmann: bullies, thugs, torturers, killers—what company!

Besides, I am too tired. Tired beyond cause, tired as an armor against the times, yearning to close my eyes, to sleep. What is death, after all, but an ascent into the final reaches of tiredness?

I remember your last telephone call. "How are you feeling?" you asked. "Tired but otherwise well," I replied. "I am taking things slowly. Florence is a pillar of strength, as ever, and I have a new man to help in the garden." "I'm so glad," you said in your brisk American voice. "You must rest a lot and concentrate on getting your strength back."

Mother and daughter on the telephone. Midday there, evening here. Summer there, winter here. Yet the line as clear as if you were next door. Our words taken apart, hurled through the skies, put together again whole, flawless. No longer the old undersea cable linking you to me but an efficient, abstract, skyborne connection: the idea of you connected to the idea of me; not words, not living breath passing between us, but the ideas of words, the idea of breath, coded, transmitted, decoded. At the end you said, "Good night, Mother," and I, "Good-bye, my dear, thank you for phoning," on the word *dear* allowing my voice to rest (what self-indulgence!) with the full weight of my love, praying that the ghost of that love would survive the cold trails of space and come home to you.

On the telephone, love but not truth. In this letter from elsewhere (so long a letter!), truth and love together at last. In every *you* that I pen love flickers and trembles like Saint Elmo's fire; you are with me not as you are today in America, not as you were when you left, but as you are in some deeper and unchanging form: as the beloved, as that which does not die. It is the soul of you that I address, as it is the soul of me that will be left with you when this letter is over. Like a moth from its case emerging, fanning its wings: that is what, reading, I hope you will glimpse: my soul readying itself for further flight. A white moth, a ghost emerging from the mouth of the figure on the deathbed. This struggling with sickness, the gloom and self-loathing of these days, the vacillation, the rambling too (there is little more to tell about the Hout Bay episode— Vercueil returned drunk and bad-tempered, found the key, and drove me home, and that was that; perhaps, if the truth be known, his dog led him back)—all part of the metamorphosis, part of shaking myself loose from the dying envelope.

And after that, after the dying? Never fear, I will not haunt you. There will be no need to close the windows and seal the chimney to keep the white moth from flapping in during the night and settling on your brow or on the brow of one of the children. The moth is simply what will brush your cheek ever so lightly as you put down the last page of this letter, before it flutters off on its next journey. It is not my soul that will remain with you but the spirit of my soul, the breath, the stirring of the air about these words, the faintest of turbulence traced in the air by the ghostly passage of my pen over the paper your fingers now hold.

Letting go of myself, letting go of you, letting go of a house still alive with memories: a hard task, but I am learning. The music too. But the music I will take with me, that at least, for it is wound into my soul. The ariosos from the Matthew Passion, wound in and knotted a thousand times, so that no one, nothing can undo them.

If Vercueil does not send these writings on, you will never read them. You will never even know they existed. A certain body of truth will never take on flesh: my truth: how I lived in these times, in this place.

What is the wager, then, that I am making with Vercueil, on Vercueil?

It is a wager on trust. So little to ask, to take a package to the post office and pass it over the counter. So little that it is almost nothing. Between taking the package and not taking it the difference is as light as a feather. If there is the slightest breath of trust, obligation, piety left behind when I am gone, he will surely take it.

And if not?

If not, there is no trust and we deserve no better, all of us, than to fall into a hole and vanish.

Because I cannot trust Vercueil I must trust him.

I am trying to keep a soul alive in times not hospitable to the soul.

Easy to give alms to the orphaned, the destitute, the hungry. Harder to give alms to the bitter-hearted (I think of Florence). But the alms I give Vercueil are hardest of all. What I give he does not forgive me for giving. No charity in him, no forgiveness. *(Charity?* says Vercueil. *Forgiveness?)* Without his forgiveness I give without charity, serve without love. Rain falling on barren soil.

When I was younger I might have given myself to him bodily. That is the sort of thing one does, one did, however mistakenly. Now I put my life in his hands instead. This is my life, these words, these tracings of the movements of crabbed digits over the page. These words, as you read them, if you read them, enter you and draw breath again. They are, if you like, my way of living on. Once upon a time you lived in me as once upon a time I lived in my mother; as she still lives in me, as I grow toward her, may I live in you.

I give my life to Vercueil to carry over. I trust Vercueil because I do not trust Vercueil. I love him because I do not love him. Because he is the weak reed I lean upon him.

I may seem to understand what I say, but, believe me, I do not. From the beginning, when I found him behind the garage in his cardboard house, sleeping, waiting, I have understood nothing. I am feeling my way along a passage that grows darker all the time. I am feeling my way toward you; with each word I feel my way.

Days ago I caught a cold, which has now settled on my chest and turned into a dry, hammering cough that goes on for minutes at a stretch and leaves me panting, exhausted.

As long as the burden is a burden of pain alone I bear it by holding it at a distance. It is not I who am in pain, I say to myself: the one in pain is someone else, some body else who shares this bed with me. So, by a trick, I hold it off, keep it elsewhere. And when the trick will not work, when the pain insists on owning me, I bear it anyhow.

(As the waves rise I have no doubt my tricks will be swept away like the dikes of Zeeland.)

But now, during these spasms of coughing, I cannot keep any distance from myself. There is no mind, there is no body, there is just I, a creature thrashing about, struggling for air, drowning. Terror, and the ignominy of terror! Another vale to be passed through on the way to death. *How can this be happening to me?* I think at the height of the coughing: *Is it fair?* The ignominy of naïveté. Even a dog with a broken back breathing its last at the roadside would not think, *But is this fair?*

Living, said Marcus Aurelius, calls for the art of the wrestler, not the dancer. Staying on your feet is all; there is no need for pretty steps.

Yesterday, with the pantry bare, I had to go shopping. Trudging home with my bags, I had a bad spell. Three passing schoolboys stopped to stare at the old woman leaning against a lamppost with her groceries spilled around her feet. In between the coughing I tried to wave them away. What I looked like I cannot imagine. A woman in a car slowed down. "Are you all right?" she called. "I have been shopping," I panted. "What?" she said, frowning, straining to hear. "Nothing!" I gasped. She drove off.

How ugly we are growing, from being unable to think well of ourselves! Even the beauty queens look irritable. Ugliness: what is it but the soul showing through the flesh?

Then last night the worst happened. Into the confusion of

my drugged, unsavory slumber penetrated the sound of bark-ing. On and on it went, steady, relentless, mechanical. Why did Vercueil not put a stop to it?

I did not trust myself on the stairs. In bathrobe and slippers I went out onto the balcony. It was cold, a light rain was falling. "Mr. Vercueil!" I croaked. "What is the dog barking about? Mr. Vercueil!"

The barking stopped, then started again. Vercueil did not appear.

I went back to bed and lay there unable to sleep, the barking like hammering in my ears.

This is how old women fall and break their hips, I warned myself: this is how the trap is laid, and this is how they are caught.

Holding on to the banister with both hands I crept down-stairs.

There was someone in the kitchen and it was not Vercueil. Whoever it was did not try to hide. My God, I thought: Bheki! A chill ran through me.

In the eerie light cast by the open refrigerator he confronted me, his forehead with the bullet wound covered by a white bandage.

"What do you want?" I whispered. "Do you want food?"

He spoke: "Where is Bheki?"

The voice was lower, thicker than Bheki's. Who could it be then? Befuddled, I searched for a name.

He closed the refrigerator door. Now we were in darkness. "Mr. Vercueil!" I croaked. The dog barked without letup. "The neighbors will come," I whispered.

As he passed me his shoulder brushed mine. Flinching, I smelled him and knew who he was.

He reached the door. The barking grew frantic.

"Florence isn't here anymore," I said. I turned on the light.

He was not wearing his own clothes. Or perhaps it is a fashion. The jacket seemed to belong to a full-grown man and the trousers were too long. One arm of the jacket was empty.

"How is your arm?" I asked.

"I must not move the arm," he said.

"Come away from the door," I said.

I opened the door a crack. The dog leapt excitedly. I tapped it on the nose. "Stop it at once!" I commanded. It whined softly. "Where is your master?" It cocked its ears. I closed the door.

"What do you want here?" I asked the boy.

"Where is Bheki?"

"Bheki is dead. He was killed last week while you were in hospital. He was shot. He died at once. The day after that affair with the bicycle."

He licked his lips. There was a cornered, uncertain look about him.

"Do you want something to eat?"

He shook his head. "Money. I have no money," he said. "For the bus."

"I will give you money. But where do you intend to go?"

"I must go home."

"Don't do that, I urge you. I know what I am talking about, I have seen what is happening on the Flats. Stay away till things have gone back to normal."

"Things will never be normal—"

"Please! I know the argument, I haven't the time or interest to go through it again. Stay here till things are quieter. Stay till you are better. Why did you leave the hospital? Are you discharged?"

"Yes. I am discharged."

"Whose clothes are you wearing?"

"They are mine."

"They are not your clothes. Where did you get them?"

"They are mine. A friend brought them to me."

He was lying. He lied no better than any other fifteen-year-old.

"Sit down. I will give you something to eat, then you can get some sleep. Wait till morning before you make up your mind what to do next."

I made tea. He sat down, paying me no attention at all. It did not embarrass him that I did not believe his story. What I believed was of no account. What did he think of me? Did he give me any thought? Was he a thinking person? No: compared with Bheki he was unthinking, inarticulate, un-imaginative. But he was alive and Bheki was dead. The lively ones are picked off, the stolid ones survive. Bheki too quick for his own good. I was never afraid of Bheki; as for this one, I am not so sure.

I put a sandwich and a cup of tea in front of him. "Eat, drink," I said. He did not stir. With his head on his arm, his eyes rolled back, he was fast asleep. I patted his cheek. "Wake up!" I said. He gave a start, sat straight, took a bite, and chewed rapidly. Then the chewing slowed. His mouth full, he sat in a stupor of exhaustion. I took the sandwich out of his hand, thinking: When they are in trouble they come to a woman. To Florence he comes, except that there is no Florence. Has he no mother of his own?

In Florence's room he recovered briefly. "The bicycle," he mumbled.

"It is safe, I have kept it. It must be fixed, that is all. I will ask Mr. Vercueil to look at it."

So this house that was once my home and yours becomes a house of refuge, a house of transit.

My dearest child, I am in a fog of error. The hour is late and I do not know how to save myself. As far as I can confess, to you I confess. What is my error, you ask? If I could put it in a bottle, like a spider, and send it to you to examine, I would do so. But it is like a fog, everywhere and nowhere. I cannot touch it, trap it, put a name to it. Slowly, reluctantly, however, let me say the first word. I do not love this child, the child sleeping in Florence's bed. I love you but I do not love him. There is no ache in me toward him, not the slightest.

Yes, you reply, he is not lovable. But did you not have a part in making him unlovable?

I do not deny that. But at the same time I do not believe it. My heart does not accept him as mine: it is as simple as that. In my heart I want him to go away and leave me alone.

That is my first word, my first confession. I do not want to die in the state I am in, in a state of ugliness. I want to be saved. How shall I be saved? By doing what I do not want to do. That is the first step: that I know. I must love, first of all, the unlovable. I must love, for instance, this child. Not bright little Bheki, but this one. He is here for a reason. He is part of my salvation. I must love him. But I do not love him. Nor do I want to love him enough to love him despite myself.

It is because I do not with a full enough heart want to be otherwise that I am still wandering in a fog.

I cannot find it in my heart to love, to want to love, to want to want to love.

I am dying because in my heart I do not want to live. I am dying because I want to die.

Therefore let me utter my second, dubious word. Not wanting to love him, how true can I say my love is for you? For love is not like hunger. Love is never sated, stilled. When one loves, one loves more. The more I love you, the more I ought to love him. The less I love him, the less, perhaps, I love you.

Cruciform logic, which takes me where I do not want to go! But would I let myself be nailed upon it if I truly were not willing?

I thought, when I began this long letter, that its pull would be as strong as the tide's, that beneath the waves beating this way and that on its surface there would be a tug as constant as the moon's drawing you to me and me to you: the blood tug of daughter to mother, woman to woman. But with every day I add to it the letter seems to grow more abstract, more abstracted, the kind of letter one writes from the stars, from the farther void, disembodied, crystalline, bloodless. Is that to be the fate of my love?

I remember, when the boy was hurt, how abundantly he bled, how rudely. How thin, by comparison, my bleeding onto the paper here. The issue of a shrunken heart.

I have written about blood before, I know. I have written about everything, I am written out, bled dry, and still I go on. This letter has become a maze, and I a dog in the maze, scurrying up and down the branches and tunnels, scratching and whining at the same old places, tiring, tired. Why do I not call for help, call to God? Because God cannot help me.

God is looking for me but he cannot reach me. God is another dog in another maze. I smell God and God smells me. I am the bitch in her time, God the male. God smells me, he can think of nothing else but finding me and taking me. Up and down the branches he bounds, scratching at the mesh. But he is lost as I am lost.

I dream, but I doubt that it is God I dream of. When I fall asleep there commences a restless movement of shapes behind my eyelids, shapes without body or form, covered in a haze, gray or brown, sulfurous. *Borodino* is the word that comes to me in my sleep: a hot summer afternoon on the Russian plain, smoke everywhere, the grass dry and burning, two hosts that have lost all cohesion plodding about, parched, in terror of their lives. Hundreds of thousands of men, faceless, voiceless, dry as bones, trapped on a field of slaughter, repeating night after night their back-and-forth march across that scorched plain in the stench of sulfur and blood: a hell into which I plummet when I close my eyes.

I am more than half convinced it is the red pills, Diconal, that call up these armies inside me. But without the red pills I can no longer sleep.

Borodino, Diconal: I stare at the words. Are they anagrams? They look like anagrams. But for what, and in what language?

When I wake out of the Borodino sleep I am calling or crying or coughing with sounds that come from deep in my chest. Then I quiet down and lie staring about me. My room, my house, my life: too close a rendering to be an imitation: the real thing: I am back: again and again I am back, from the belly of the whale disgorged. A miracle each time, unacknowledged, uncelebrated, unwelcome. Morning after morning I am disgorged, cast up on the shore, given another chance. And what do I do with it? Lie without motion on the sands waiting for the night tide to return, to encircle me, to bear me back into the belly of darkness. Not properly born: a liminal creature, unable to breathe in water, that lacks the courage to leave the sea behind and become a dweller on land.

At the airport, the day you left, you gripped me and stared into my eyes. "Do not call me back, Mother," you said, "because I will not come." Then you shook the dust of this country from your feet. You were right. Nevertheless, there is part of me that is always on the alert, always turned to the northwest, longing to welcome you, embrace you, should you relent and, in whatever form, come visiting. There is something as terrible as it is admirable in that will of yours, in the letters you write in which—let me be candid—there is not enough love, or at least not enough of the loving-yielding that brings love to life. Affectionate, kind, confiding even, full of concern for me, they are nonetheless the letters of someone grown strange, estranged.

Is this an accusation? No, but it is a reproach, a heartfelt reproach. And this long letter—I say it now—is a call into the night, into the northwest, for you to come back to me. Come and bury your head in my lap as a child does, as you used to, your nose burrowing like a mole's for the place you came from. Come, says this letter: do not cut yourself off from me. My third word.

If you would say you came from me, I would not have to say I came from the belly of the whale.

I cannot live without a child. I cannot die without a child.

What I bear, in your absence, is pain. I produce pain. You are my pain.

Is this an accusation? Yes. *J'accuse.* I accuse you of abandoning me. I fling this accusation at you, into the northwest, into the teeth of the wind. I fling my pain at you.

Borodino: an anagram for *Come back* in some language or other. Diconal: *I call.*

Words vomited up from the belly of the whale, misshapen, mysterious. Daughter.

In the middle of the night I telephoned Lifeline. "Home deliveries?" said the woman. "I don't know of anyone who does home deliveries anymore except Stuttafords. Would you like to try Meals on Wheels?"

"It is not a question of cooking," I said. "I can do my own cooking. I just want the groceries delivered. I am having difficulty carrying things."

"Give me your number and I'll get a social worker to phone you in the morning," she said.

I put down the receiver.

The end comes galloping. I had not reckoned that as one goes downhill one goes faster and faster. I thought the whole road could be taken at an amble. Wrong, quite wrong.

There is something degrading about the way it all ends— degrading not only to us but to the idea we have of ourselves, of humankind. People lying in dark bedrooms, in their own mess, helpless. People lying in hedges in the rain. You will not understand this, yet. Vercueil will.

Vercueil has disappeared again, leaving the dog behind. A pity about Vercueil. No Odysseus, no Hermes, perhaps not even a messenger. A circler-around. A ditherer, despite the weatherworn front.

And I? If Vercueil has failed his test, what was mine? Was

my test whether I had the courage to incinerate myself in front of the House of Lies? I have gone over that moment a thousand times in my mind, the moment of striking the match when my ears are softly buffeted and I sit astonished and even pleased in the midst of the flames, untouched, my clothes burning without singeing, the flames a cool blue. *How easy to give meaning to one's life,* I think with surprise, thinking very fast in the last instant before the eyelashes catch, and the eyebrows, and one no longer sees. Then after that no thought anymore, only pain (for nothing comes without its price).

Would the pain be worse than toothache? Than childbirth? Than this hip? Than childbirth multiplied by two? How many Diconal to mute it? Would it be playing the game to swallow all the Diconal before turning the car down Government Avenue, edging past the chain? Must one die in full knowledge, fully oneself? Must one give birth to one's death without anesthetic?

The truth is, there was always something false about that impulse, deeply false, no matter to what rage or despair it answered. If dying in bed over weeks and months, in a purgatory of pain and shame, will not save my soul, why should I be saved by dying in two minutes in a pillar of flames? Will the lies stop because a sick old woman kills herself? Whose life will be changed, and how? I go back to Florence, as so often. If Florence were passing by, with Hope at her side and Beauty on her back, would she be impressed by the spectacle? Would she even spare it a glance? A juggler, a clown, an entertainer, Florence would think: not a serious person. And stride on.

What would count in Florence's eyes as a serious death? What would win her approval? Answer: a death that crowns a life of honorable labor; or else that comes of itself, irresistible, unannounced, like a clap of thunder, like a bullet between the eyes.

Florence is the judge. Behind the glasses her eyes are still, measuring all. A stillness she has already passed on to her daughters. The court belongs to Florence; it is I who pass under review. If the life I live is an examined life, it is because for ten years I have been under examination in the court of Florence.

"Have you got Dettol?"

His voice startled me as I sat in the kitchen writing. His, the boy's.

"Go upstairs. Look in the bathroom, the door on the right. Look in the cupboard under the basin."

There were splashing noises, then he came down again. The bandage was off; with surprise I noticed that the stitches were still in.

"Didn't they take out the stitches?"

He shook his head.

"But when did you leave the hospital?"

"Yesterday. The day before yesterday."

Why the need to lie?

"Why didn't you stay and let them take care of you?"

No response.

"You must keep that cut covered, otherwise it will get infected and leave you with a scar." With a mark like a whiplash across his forehead for the rest of his life. A memento.

Who is he to me that I should nag him? Yet I held closed his open flesh, staunched the flow of his blood. How persistent the impulse to mother! As a hen that loses its chicks will take in a duckling, oblivious of the yellow fur, the flat beak, and teach it to take sand baths, peck at worms.

I shook out the red tablecloth and began to cut it. "I don't have any bandages in the house," I said, "but this is quite clean, if you don't mind red." Around his head I wound a strip twice and knotted it behind. "You must go to a doctor soon, or a clinic, to have the stitches taken out. You can't leave them in."

His neck stiff as a poker. A smell coming from him, the smell that must have set the dog off: nervousness, fear.

"My head is not sore," he said, clearing his throat, "but my arm"—he moved his shoulder gingerly—"I must rest my arm."

"Tell me, are you running away from someone?"

He was silent.

"I want to speak to you seriously," I said. "You are too young for this kind of thing. I told Bheki so and I tell you again. You must listen to me. I am an old person, I know what I am talking about. You are still children. You are throwing away your lives before you know what life can be. What are you—fifteen years old? Fifteen is too young to die. Eighteen is too young. Twenty-one is too young."

He got up, brushing the red band with his fingertips. A favor. In the age of chivalry men hacked other men to death with women's favors fluttering on their helmets. A waste of breath to preach prudence to this boy. The instinct for battle too strong in him, driving him on. Battle: nature's way of liquidating the weak and providing mates for the strong. Return covered in glory, and you shall have your desire. Gore and glory, death and sex. And I, an old woman, crone of death, tying a favor around his head!

"Where is Bheki?" he said.

I searched his face. Had he not understood what I told him? Had he forgotten? "Sit down," I said.

He sat.

I leaned across the table. "Bheki is in the ground," I said. "He is in a box in a hole with earth heaped on top of him. He is never going to leave that hole. Never, never, never. Understand: this is not a game like football, where after you fall down you get up and go on playing. The men you are playing against don't say to each other, 'That one is just a child, let us shoot a child's bullet at him, a play bullet.' They don't think of you as a child at all. They think of you as the enemy and they hate you quite as much as you hate them. They will have no qualms about shooting you; on the contrary, they will smile with pleasure when you fall and make another notch on their gunstocks."

He stared back at me as if I were striking him in the face, blow after blow. But, jaw set, lips clenched, he refused to wince. Over his eyes that smoky film.

"You think their discipline is poor," I said. "You are wrong. Their discipline is very good. What holds them back from exterminating every male child, every last one of you, is not compassion or fellow feeling. It is discipline, nothing else: orders from above, that can change any day. Compassion is flown out of the window. This is war. Listen to what I am saying! I know what I am talking about. You think I am trying to lure you out of the struggle. Well, that is true. That is what I am doing. I say: Wait, you are too young."

He shifted restlessly. Talk, talk! Talk had weighed down the generation of his grandparents and the generation of his parents. Lies, promises, blandishments, threats: they had walked stooped under the weight of all the talk. Not he. He threw off talk. Death to talk!

"You say it is time to fight," I said. "You say it is time to win or lose. Let me tell you something about that *win or lose*. Let me tell you something about that *or*. Listen to me.

"You know I am sick. Do you know what is wrong with me? I have cancer. I have cancer from the accumulation of shame I have endured in my life. That is how cancer comes about: from self-loathing the body turns malignant and begins to eat away at itself.

"You say, 'What is the point of consuming yourself in shame and loathing? I don't want to listen to the story of how you feel, it is just another story, why don't you *do* something?' And when you say that, I say, 'Yes.' I say, 'Yes.' I say, 'Yes.'

"There is nothing I can reply but 'Yes' when you put that question to me. But let me tell you what it is like to utter that 'Yes.' It is like being on trial for your life and being allowed only two words, Yes and No. Whenever you take a breath to speak out, you are warned by the judges: 'Yes or No: no speeches.' 'Yes,' you say. Yet all the time you feel other words stirring inside you like life in the womb. Not like a child kicking, not yet, but like the very beginnings, like the deep-down stirring of knowledge a woman has when she is pregnant.

"There is not only death inside me. There is life too. The death is strong, the life is weak. But my duty is to the life. I must keep it alive. I must.

"You do not believe in words. You think only blows are real, blows and bullets. But listen to me: can't you hear that the words I speak are real? Listen! They may only be air but they come from my heart, from my womb. They are not Yes, they are not No. What is living inside me is something else, another word. And I am fighting for it, in my manner, fighting for it not to be stifled. I am like one of those Chinese mothers who know that their child will be taken away from them, if it is a daughter, and done away with, because the need, the family's need, the village's need, is for sons with strong arms. They know that after the birth someone will come into the room, someone whose face will be hidden, who will take the child from the midwife's arms and, if the sex is wrong, turn his back on them, out of delicacy, and stifle it just like that, pinching the little nose to, holding the jaw shut. A minute and all is done.

"Grieve if you like, the mother is told afterward: grief is only natural. But do not ask: What is this thing called a son? What is this thing called a daughter, that it must die?

"Do not misunderstand me. You are a son, somebody's son. I am not against sons. But have you ever seen a newborn baby? Let me tell you, you would find it hard to tell the difference between boy and girl. Every baby has the same puffy-looking fold between the legs. The spout, the tendril that is said to mark out the boy is no great thing, really. Very little to make the difference between life and death. Yet everything else, everything indefinite, everything that gives when you press it, is condemned unheard. I am arguing for that unheard.

"You are tired of listening to old people, I can see. You are itching to be a man and do a man's things. You are tired of getting ready for life. It is time for life itself, you think. What an error you are making! Life is not following a stick, a pole, a flagstaff, a gun, and seeing where it will take you. Life is not around the corner. You are already in the midst of life."

The telephone rang.

"It's all right, I am not going to answer it," I said.

In silence we waited for the ringing to stop.

"I don't know your name," I said.

"John."

John: a *nom de guerre* if ever I heard one.

"What are your plans?"

He looked uncomprehending.

"What do you plan to do? Do you want to stay here?"

"I must go home."

"Where is home?"

He stared back at me doggedly, too tired to think up another lie. "Poor child," I whispered.

I did not mean to spy. But I was wearing slippers, the door to Florence's room was open, his back was to me. He was sitting on the bed, intent on some object he had in his hand. When he heard me he gave a start and thrust it beneath the bedclothes.

"What is it you have there?" I asked.

"It is nothing," he said, giving me one of his forced stares.

I would not have pressed him had I not noticed that a length of baseboard had been prized from the wall and lay on the floor, revealing unplastered brickwork.

"What are you up to?" I said. "Why are you pulling the room to pieces?"

He was silent.

"Show me what you are hiding."

He shook his head.

I peered at the wall. There was a gap in the brickwork where a ventilator had been let in; through the gap one could reach under the floorboards.

"Are you putting things under the floor?"

"I am not doing anything."

I dialed the number Florence had left. A child answered. "Can I speak to Mrs. Mkubukeli," I said. Silence. "Mrs. Mkubukeli. Florence."

Murmurs, then a woman's voice: "Who do you want to speak to?"

"Mrs. Mkubukeli. Florence."

"She is not here."

"This is Mrs. Curren," I said. "Mrs. Mkubukeli used to work for me. I am phoning about her son's friend, the boy who calls himself John, I don't know his real name. It is important. If Florence is not there, can I speak to Mr. Thabane?"

Again a long silence. Then a man's voice: "Yes, this is Thabane."

"This is Mrs. Curren. You remember, we met. I am phoning about Bheki's friend, from his school. Perhaps you don't know, but he has been in hospital."

"I know."

"Now he has left the hospital, or run away, and come here. I have reason to believe he has a weapon of some kind, I don't know what exactly, which he and Bheki must have hidden in Florence's room. I think that is why he has come back."

"Yes," he said flatly.

"Mr. Thabane, I am not asking you to assert authority over the boy. But he is not well. He was quite badly injured. And I think he is in an emotionally disturbed state. I don't know how to get in touch with his family, I don't even know whether he has family in Cape Town. He won't tell me. All I am asking is that someone should come and talk to him, someone he trusts, and take him away before something happens to him."

"He is in an emotionally disturbed state. What do you mean?"

"I mean he needs help. I mean he may not be responsible for his actions. I mean he has had a blow to the head. I mean I cannot take care of him, it is beyond me. Someone must come."

"I will see."

"No, that is not good enough. I want an undertaking."

"I will ask someone to fetch him. But I cannot tell you when."

"Today?"

"I cannot say today. Perhaps today, perhaps tomorrow. I will see."

"Mr. Thabane, let me make one thing clear to you. I am not trying to prescribe to this boy or to anyone else what he should do with his life. He is old enough and self-willed enough to do what he will do. But as for this killing, this bloodletting in the name of *comradeship,* I detest it with all my heart and soul. I think it is barbarous. That is what I want to say."

"This is not a good line, Mrs. Curren. Your voice is very tiny, very tiny and very far away. I hope you can hear me."

"I can hear you."

"Good. Then let me say, Mrs. Curren, I don't think you understand very much about comradeship."

"I understand enough, thank you."

"No, you don't," he said, quite certain of himself. "When you are body and soul in the struggle as these young people are, when you are prepared to lay down your lives for each other without question, then a bond grows up that is stronger than any bond you will know again. That is comradeship. I see it every day with my own eyes. My generation has nothing that can compare. That is why we must stand back for them, for the youth. We stand back but we stand behind them. That is what you cannot understand, because you are too far away."

"I am far away, certainly," I said, "far away and tiny. Nevertheless, I fear I know comradeship all too well. The Germans had comradeship, and the Japanese, and the Spartans. Shaka's impis too, I am sure. Comradeship is nothing but a mystique of death, of killing and dying, masquerading as what you call a bond (a bond of what? Love? I doubt it). I have no sympathy with this comradeship. You are wrong, you and Florence and everyone else, to be taken in by it and, worse, to encourage it in children. It is just another of those icy, exclusive, death-driven male constructions. That is my opinion."

More passed between us, but I won't repeat it. We exchanged opinions. We agreed to differ.

The afternoon dragged on. No one came to fetch the boy. I lay in bed, groggy with drugs, a cushion under my back, trying with one small adjustment after another to ease the pain, longing for sleep, dreading the dream of Borodino.

The air thickened, it began to rain. From the blocked gutter came a steady drip. The smell of cat urine wafted in from the carpet on the landing. A tomb, I thought: a late bourgeois tomb. My head turned this way and that. Gray hair on the pillow, unwashed, lank. And in Florence's room, in the growing dark, the boy, lying on his back with the bomb or whatever it is in his hand, his eyes wide open, not veiled now but clear: thinking, more than thinking, envisioning. Envisioning the moment of glory when he will arise, fully himself at last, erect, powerful, transfigured. When the fiery flower will unfold, when the pillar of smoke will rise. The bomb on his chest like a talisman: as Christopher Columbus lay in the dark of his cabin, holding the compass to his chest, the mystic instrument that would guide him to the Indies, the Isles of the Blest. Troops of maidens with bared breasts singing to him, opening their arms, as he wades to them through the shallows holding before him the needle that never wavers, that points forever in one direction, to the future.

Poor child! Poor child! From somewhere tears sprang and blurred my sight. Poor John, who in the old days would have been destined to be a garden boy and eat bread and jam for lunch at the back door and drink out of a tin, battling now for all the insulted and injured, the trampled, the ridiculed, for all the garden boys of South Africa!

In the cold early morning I heard the gate to the courtyard being tried. Vercueil, I thought: Vercueil is back. Then the doorbell rang, once, twice, long rings, peremptory, impatient, and I knew it was not Vercueil.

It takes me minutes nowadays to get downstairs, particularly if I am befuddled by the pills. While I crept down in the half-dark they went on ringing the bell, rapping at the door. "I am coming!" I called as loudly as I could. But I was too slow. I heard the courtyard gate swing open. There was a burst of knocking at the kitchen door, and voices speaking Afrikaans. Then, as flat and unremarkable as one stone striking another, came the sound of a shot.

A silence fell in which I clearly heard the tinkle of breaking glass. "Wait!" I called, and ran, truly ran—I did not know I had it in me—to the kitchen door. "Wait!" I called, slapping at the pane, fumbling with the bolts and chains. "Don't do anything!"

There was someone in a blue overcoat standing on the veranda with his back to me. Though he must have heard me, he did not turn.

I drew the last bolt, flung the door open, appeared among them. I had forgotten my gown, my feet were bare, I stood there in my white nightdress like, for all I know, a body risen from the dead. "Wait!" I said. "Don't do anything yet, he is just a child!"

There were three of them. Two were in uniform. The third, wearing a pullover with reindeer running in a band across his chest, held a pistol pointing downward. "Give me a chance to talk to him," I said, splashing through the night's puddles. They stared in astonishment but did not try to stop me.

The window of Florence's room was shattered. The room itself was in darkness; but, peering through the hole, I could make out a figure crouched beside the bed at the far end.

"Open the door, my boy," I said. "I won't let them hurt you, I promise."

It was a lie. He was lost, I had no power to save him. Yet something went out from me to him. I ached to embrace him, to protect him.

One of the policemen appeared beside me, pressed against the wall. "Tell him to come out," he said. I turned on him in a fury. "Go away!" I screamed, and fell into a fit of coughing.

The sun was coming up, rosy, in a sky full of drifting cloud.

"John!" I called through the coughing. "Come out! I will not let them do anything to you."

Now the man in the pullover was at my side. "Tell him to pass out his weapons," he said in a low voice.

"What weapons?"

"He has a pistol, I don't know what else. Tell him to pass everything out."

"First promise you will not hurt him."

His fingers closed on my arm. I resisted, but he was too strong. "You are going to catch pneumonia out here," he said. Something descended on me from behind: a coat, an overcoat, one of the policemen's overcoats. *"Neem haar binne,"* he murmured. They guided me back to the kitchen and closed the door on me.

I sat down, stood up again. The coat stank of cigarette smoke. I dropped it on the floor and opened the door. My feet were blue with cold. "John!" I called. The three men were huddled over a radio. The one who had given me his coat turned with an exasperated air. "Lady, it is dangerous out here," he said. He bundled me indoors again, then could not find the key to lock the door.

"He is just a child," I said.

"Let us do our work, lady," he replied.

"I am watching you," I said. "I am watching everything you do. I tell you, he is just a child!"

He drew a breath as though about to respond, then let it out in a sigh and waited for me to talk myself out. A young man, solid, raw-boned. Son to someone, cousin to many. Many cousins, many aunts and uncles, great-aunts and great-uncles, standing about him, behind him, above him like a chorus, guiding, admonishing.

What could I say? What did we have in common to make intercourse possible, except that he was here to defend me, to defend my interests, in the wider sense?

"Ek staan nie aan jou kant nie," I said. *"Ek staan aan die*

teenkant." I stand on the other side. But on the other bank too, the other bank of the river. On the far bank, looking back.

He turned, inspecting the stove, the sink, the racks, occupying *die ou dame* while his friends did their business outside. All in a day's work.

"That's all," I said. "I'm finished. I wasn't talking to you anyway."

To whom then? To you: always to you. How I live, how I lived: my story.

The doorbell rang. More men, men in boots and caps and camouflage uniforms, tramping through the house. They clustered at the kitchen window. *"Hy sit daar in die buitekamer,"* explained the policeman, pointing to Florence's room. *"Daar's net die een deur en die een venster."*

"Nee, dan het ons hom," said one of the newcomers.

"I warn you, I'm watching everything you do," I said.

He turned to me. "Do you know this boy?" he said.

"Yes, I know him."

"Did you know he had arms?"

I shrugged. "God save the unarmed in these days."

Someone else came in, a young woman in uniform with a crisp, clean air about her. *"Is dit die dame dié?"* she said; and then, to me: "We are going to clear the house for a little while, till this business is over. Is there anywhere you would like to go, friends or relatives?"

"I am not leaving. This is my house."

Her friendliness, her concern did not waver. "I know," she said, "but it's too dangerous to stay. For just a little while we must ask you to leave."

The men at the window had stopped talking now: they were impatient for me to be gone. *"Bel die ambulans,"* said one of them. *"Ag, sy kan sommer by die stasie wag,"* said the woman. She turned to me. "Come now, Mrs. . . ." She waited for me to supply the name. I did not. "A nice warm cup of tea," she offered.

"I am not going."

They paid my words no more attention than they would a child's. *"Gaan haal 'n kombers,"* said the man, *"sy's amper blou van die koue."*

The woman went upstairs and came back with the quilt from my bed. She wrapped it around me, gave me a hug, then helped me into my slippers. No sign of disgust at my legs, my feet. A good girl, reared to make someone a good wife.

"Are there any pills or medicines or anything else you want to take along?" she asked.

"I'm not leaving," I repeated, gripping my chair.

Murmured words passed between her and the men. Without warning I was lifted from behind, under the arms. The woman took my legs. Like a carpet they carried me to the front door. Pain racked my back. "Put me down!" I cried.

"In a minute," said the woman soothingly.

"I have cancer!" I screamed. *"Put me down!"*

Cancer! What a pleasure to fling the word at them! It stopped them in their tracks like a knife. *"Sit haar neer, dalk kom haar iets oor,"* said the man holding me. *"Ek het mos gesê jy moet die ambulans bel."* Gingerly they laid me down on the sofa.

"Where is the pain?" asked the woman, frowning.

"In my heart," I said. She looked puzzled. "I have cancer of the heart." Then she understood; she shook her head as if shaking off flies.

"Does it pain you to be carried?"

"It pains me all the time," I said.

She caught the eye of the man behind me; something passed between them so amusing that she could not keep back a smile.

"I caught it by drinking from the cup of bitterness," I plunged on. What did it matter if they thought me dotty? "You will probably catch it too one day. It is hard to escape."

There was a crash of breaking glass. Both of them rushed from the room; I got up and limped behind.

Nothing had changed except that a second windowpane was gone. The courtyard itself was empty; the policemen, half a dozen of them now, were crouching on the veranda, guns at the ready.

"Weg!" shouted one of them furiously. *"Kry haar weg!"*

The woman bundled me indoors. As she closed the door there was a curt explosion, a fusillade of shots, then a long stunned silence, then low talk and, from somewhere, the sound of Vercueil's dog yapping.

I tried to pull open the door, but the woman held me tight.

"If you have hurt him I will never forgive you," I said.

"It's all right, we'll phone again for the ambulance," she said, trying to soothe me.

But the ambulance was already there, drawn up on the sidewalk. Scores of people were gathering excitedly from all directions, neighbors, passersby, young and old, black and white; from the balconies of the flats people stared down. By the time the policewoman and I emerged from the front door they were wheeling the body, covered in a blanket, down the driveway, and loading it aboard.

I made to climb into the ambulance after it; one of the attendants even took my arm to help me in; but a policeman intervened. "Wait, we'll send another ambulance for her," he said.

"I don't want another ambulance," I said. He put on a kindly, nonplussed look. "I want to go with him," I said, and made another attempt to climb in. The quilt fell to my feet.

He shook his head. "No," he said. He gestured and the attendant closed the doors.

"God forgive us!" I breathed. With the quilt clasped around me I began to walk down Schoonder Street, away from the crowd. I had almost reached the corner when the policewoman came trotting after me. "You must come home now!" she ordered. "It's not my home anymore," I replied in a fury, and kept walking. She took my arm; I shook myself free. *"Sy's van haar kop af,"* she remarked to no one in particular, and gave up.

In Buitenkant Street, under the overpass, I sat down to rest. A steady stream of cars flowed past, heading for the city. No one spared me a glance. With my wild hair and pink quilt I might be a spectacle on Schoonder Street; here, amid the rubble and filth, I was just part of the urban shadowland.

A man and woman passed on foot on the other side of the street. Did I recognize the woman? Was it the one Vercueil had brought to the house, or did all the women who hung around the Avalon Hotel and Solly Kramer's Liquor Store have those wasted, spidery legs? The man, carrying a knotted plastic bag over his shoulder, was not Vercueil.

I wrapped myself tighter in the quilt and lay down. Through my bones I could feel the rumble of traffic on the overpass. The pills were in the house, the house in other hands. Could I survive without the pills? No. But did I want to survive? I was beginning to feel the indifferent peace of an old animal that, sensing its time is near, creeps, cold and sluggish, into the hole in the ground where everything will contract to the slow thudding of a heart. Behind a concrete pillar, in a place where the sun had not shone for thirty years, I curled up on my good side, listening to the beat of the pain that might as well have been the beat of my pulse.

I must have slept. Time must have passed. When I opened my eyes there was a child kneeling beside me, feeling inside the folds of the quilt. His hand crept over my body. "There is nothing for you," I tried to say, but my teeth were loose. Ten years old at most, with a shaven skull and bare feet and a hard look. Behind him two companions, even younger. I slipped out the teeth. "Leave me alone," I said. "I am sick, you will get sick from me."

Slowly they withdrew and, like crows, stood waiting.

I had to empty my bladder. Yielding, I urinated where I lay. Thank God for the cold, I thought, thank God for the numbness: all things work together toward an easy birth.

The boys came closer again. I awaited the prying of their hands, not caring. The roar of wheels lulled me; like a grub in a hive, I was absorbed into the hum of the spinning world. The air dense with noise. Thousands of wings passing and repassing without touching. How was there space for them all? How is there space in the skies for the souls of all the departed? Because, says Marcus Aurelius, they fuse one with another: they burn and fuse and so are returned to the great cycle.

Death after death. Bee ash.

The flap of the quilt was drawn back. I felt light on my eyelids, coldness too on my cheeks where the tears had run. Something pressed between my lips, was forced between my gums. I gagged and pulled away. All three children were clustered over me now in the gloom; there may have been others too, behind them. What were they doing? I tried to push the hand away but it pressed all the harder. An ugly noise came from my throat, a dry rasp like wood splitting. The hand withdrew. "Don't—" I said; but my palate was sore, it was hard to form words.

What did I want to say? *Don't do that!? Don't you see I have nothing?? Don't you have any mercy??* What nonsense. Why should there be mercy in the world? I thought of beetles, those big black beetles with the humped backs, dying, waving their legs feebly, and ants pouring over them, gnawing at the soft places, the joints, the eyes, tearing away the beetle flesh.

It was a stick, nothing more, a stick a few inches long that he had forced into my mouth. I could taste the grains of dirt it left behind.

With the tip of the stick he lifted my upper lip. I pulled back and tried to spit. Impassively he stood up. With a bare foot he kicked, and a little rain of dust and pebbles struck my face.

A car passed, outlining the children in its headlights. They began to move off down Buitenkant Street. Darkness returned.

Did these things really happen? Yes, these things happened. There is no more to be said about it. They happened a stone's throw from Breda Street and Schoonder Street and Vrede Street, where a century ago the patricians of Cape Town gave orders that there be erected spacious homes for themselves and their descendants in perpetuity, foreseeing nothing of the day when, in their shadows, the chickens would come home to roost.

There was a fog in my head, a gray confusion. I shivered;

paroxysms of yawning passed over me. For a while I was nowhere.

Then something was sniffing at my face: a dog. I tried to ward it off but it found a way past my fingers. So I yielded, thinking, there are worse things than a dog's wet nose, its eager breath. I let it lick my face, lick my lips, lick up the salt of my tears. Kisses, if one wanted to look at them that way.

Someone was with the dog. Did I recognize the smell? Was it Vercueil, or did all street wanderers smell of moldering leaves, of underwear rotting in the ash heap? "Mr. Vercueil?" I croaked, and the dog whined with excitement, giving a great sneeze straight into my face.

A match flared. Yes, it was Vercueil, hat and all. "Who put you here?" he asked. "Myself," I said, past the raw place on my palate. The match died. Tears came again, which the dog eagerly consumed.

With his high shoulder blades and his chest narrow as a gull's, I would not have guessed that Vercueil could be so strong. But he lifted me, wet patch and all, and carried me. I thought: forty years since I was last carried by a man. The misfortune of a tall woman. Will this be how the story ends: with being carried in strong arms across the sands, through the shallows, past the breakers, into the darker depths?

We were away from the overpass, in blessed stillness. How much more bearable everything was suddenly becoming! Where was the pain? Was the pain in a better humor too? "Don't go back to Schoonder Street," I ordered.

We passed under a streetlight. I saw the strain in the muscles of his neck, heard his breath coming fast. "Put me down for a minute," I said. He put me down and rested. When would the time come when the jacket fell away and great wings sprouted from his shoulders?

Up Buitenkant Street he bore me, across Vrede Street, street of peace, and, treading more slowly, groping before each step, into a dark wooded space. Through branches I glimpsed the stars.

He set me down.

"I am so happy to see you," I said, the words coming from my heart, heartfelt. And then: "I was attacked by some children before you came. Attacked or violated or explored, I don't know which. That is why I talk so strangely. They pushed a stick into my mouth, I still don't understand why. What pleasure could it have given them?"

"They wanted your gold teeth," he said. "They get money for gold from the pawnshops."

"Gold teeth? How strange. I haven't any gold teeth. I took my teeth out anyway. Here they are."

From somewhere in the dark he fetched cardboard, a carton box folded flat. He spread it and helped me to lie down. Then without haste, without ceremony, he lay down too with his back to me. The dog settled between our legs.

"Do you want some of the quilt?" I said.

"I'm OK."

Time passed.

"I'm sorry, but I'm terribly thirsty," I whispered. "Is there no water here?"

He got up and came back with a bottle. I smelled it: sweet wine, the bottle half full. "It's all I've got," he said. I drank it down. It did nothing for my thirst, but in the sky the stars began to swim. Everything grew remote: the smell of damp earth, the cold, the man beside me, my own body. Like a crab after a long day, tired, folding its claws, even the pain went to sleep. I swooped back into darkness.

When I awoke he had turned and flung an arm across my neck. I could have freed myself, but preferred not to disturb him. So while by slow degrees the new day broke, I lay face to face with him, not stirring. His eyes opened once, alert, like an animal's. "I am not gone," I murmured. The eyes closed.

The thought came: Whom, of all beings on earth, do I know best at this hour? Him. Every hair of his beard, every crease of his forehead known to me. Him, not you. Because he is here, beside me, now.

Forgive me. Time is short, I must trust my heart and tell the truth. Sightless, ignorant, I follow where the truth takes me.

"Are you awake?" I murmured.

"Yes."

"Both those boys are dead now," I said. "They have killed them both. Did you know?"

"I know."

"You know what happened at the house?"

"Yes."

"Do you mind if I talk?"

"Talk."

"Let me tell you: I met Florence's brother the day Bheki died—brother or cousin or whatever. An educated man. I told him how I wished Bheki had never got involved in—what shall I call it?—the struggle. 'He is just a child,' I said: 'He isn't ready. But for that friend of his, he would never have been drawn in.'

"Later I spoke to him again on the telephone. I told him

frankly what I thought of the comradeship for which both those children have now died. A mystique of death, I called it. I blamed people like Florence and him for doing nothing to discourage it.

"He heard me out civilly. I was entitled to my opinions, he said. I did not change his mind.

"But now I ask myself: What right have I to opinions about comradeship or anything else? What right have I to wish Bheki and his friend had kept out of trouble? To have opinions in a vacuum, opinions that touch no one, is, it seems to me, nothing. Opinions must be heard by others, heard and weighed, not merely listened to out of politeness. And to be weighed they must have weight. Mr. Thabane does not weigh what I say. It has no weight to him. Florence does not even hear me. To Florence what goes on in my head is a matter of complete indifference, I know that."

Vercueil got up, went behind a tree, urinated. Then, to my surprise, he came and lay down again. The dog snuggled against him, its nose in his crotch. With my tongue I probed the sore place in my mouth, tasting the blood.

"I have not changed my mind," I said. "I still detest these calls for sacrifice that end with young men bleeding to death in the mud. War is never what it pretends to be. Scratch the surface and you find, invariably, old men sending young men to their death in the name of some abstraction or other. Despite what Mr. Thabane says (I do not blame him, the future comes disguised, if it came naked we would be petrified by what we saw), it remains a war of the old upon the young. *Freedom or death!* shout Bheki and his friends. Whose words? Not their own. *Freedom or death!,* I have no doubt, those two little girls are rehearsing in their sleep. *No!* I want to say: *Save yourselves!*

"Whose is the true voice of wisdom, Mr. Vercueil? Mine, I believe. Yet who am I, *who am I* to have a voice at all? How can I honorably urge them to turn their back on that call? What am I entitled to do but sit in a corner with my mouth shut? I have no voice; I lost it long ago; perhaps I have never had one. I have no voice, and that is that. The rest should be silence. But with this—whatever it is—this voice that is no voice, I go on. On and on."

Was Vercueil smiling? His face was hidden. In a toothless whisper sticky with sibilants I went on.

"A crime was committed long ago. How long ago? I do not know. But longer ago than 1916, certainly. So long ago that I was born into it. It is part of my inheritance. It is part of me, I am part of it.

"Like every crime it had its price. That price, I used to think, would have to be paid in shame: in a life of shame and a shameful death, unlamented, in an obscure corner. I accepted that. I did not try to set myself apart. Though it was not a crime I asked to be committed, it was committed in my name. I raged at times against the men who did the dirty work—you have seen it, a shameful raging as *stupid* as what it raged against—but I accepted too that, in a sense, they lived inside me. So that when in my rages I wished them dead, I wished death on myself too. In the name of honor. Of an honorable notion of honor. *Honesta mors.*

"I have no idea what freedom is, Mr. Vercueil. I am sure Bheki and his friend had no idea either. Perhaps freedom is always and only what is unimaginable. Nevertheless, we know unfreedom when we see it—don't we? Bheki was not free, and knew it. You are not free, at least not on this earth, nor am I. I was born a slave and I will most certainly die a slave. A life in fetters, a death in fetters: that is part of the price, not to be quibbled at, not to be whined about.

"What I did not know, *what I did not know*—listen to me now!—was that the price was even higher. I had miscalculated. Where did the mistake come in? It had something to do with honor, with the notion I clung to through thick and thin, from my education, from my reading, that in his soul the honorable man can suffer no harm. I strove always for honor, for a private honor, using shame as my guide. As long as I was ashamed I knew I had not wandered into dishonor. That was the use of shame: as a touchstone, something that would always be there, something you could come back to like a blind person, to touch, to tell you where you were. For the rest I kept a decent distance from my shame. I did not wallow in it. Shame never became a shameful pleasure; it never ceased to gnaw me. I was not proud of it, I was ashamed of it. My shame, my own. Ashes in my mouth day after day after day, which never ceased to taste like ashes.

"It is a confession I am making here, this morning, Mr. Vercueil," I said, "as full a confession as I know how. I withhold no secrets. I have been a good person, I freely confess to it. I am a good person still. What times these are when to be a good person is not enough!

"What I had not calculated on was that more might be called for than to be good. For there are plenty of good people in this country. We are two a penny, we good and nearly good. What the times call for is quite different from goodness. The times call for heroism. A word that, as I speak it, sounds foreign to my lips. I doubt that I have ever used it before, even in a lecture. Why not? Perhaps out of respect. Perhaps out of shame. As one drops one's gaze before a naked man. I would have used the words *heroic status* instead, I think, in a lecture. The hero with his heroic status. The hero, that antique naked figure."

A deep groan came from Vercueil's throat. I craned over, but all I could see was the stubble on his cheek and a hairy ear. "Mr. Vercueil!" I whispered. He did not stir. Asleep? Pretending to sleep? How much had passed him by unheard? Had he heard about goodness and heroism? About honor and shame? Is a true confession still true if it is not heard? Do you hear me, or have I put you to sleep too?

I went behind a bush. Birds were singing all around. Who would have thought there was such birdlife in the suburbs! It was like Arcady. No wonder Vercueil and his friends lived out of doors. What is a roof good for but to keep off the rain? Vercueil and his comrades.

I lay down beside him again, my feet cold and muddy. It was quite light now. On our flattened-out box in the vacant lot we must have been visible to every passerby. That is how we must be in the eyes of the angels: people living in houses of glass, our every act naked. Our hearts naked too, beating in chests of glass. Birdsong poured down like rain.

"I feel so much better this morning," I said. "But perhaps we should go back now. Feeling better is usually a warning that I am going to feel worse."

Vercueil sat up, took off his hat, scratched his scalp with long, dirty nails. The dog came trotting up from somewhere and fussed around us. Vercueil folded the cardboard and hid it in the bushes.

"Do you know I have had a breast removed?" I said out of the blue.

He fidgeted, looked uncomfortable.

"I regret it now, of course. Regret that I am marked. It becomes like trying to sell a piece of furniture with a scratch or a burn mark. It's still a perfectly good chair, you say, but people aren't interested. People don't like marked objects. I am talking about my life. It may not be perfectly good, but it is still a life, not a half-life. I thought I would sell it or spend it to save my honor. But who will accept it in its present state? It is like trying to spend a drachma. A perfectly good coin somewhere else, but not here. Suspiciously marked.

"But I haven't quite given up yet. I am still casting around for something to do with it. Do you have any suggestions?"

Vercueil put on his hat, tugging it down firmly fore and aft.

"I would love to buy you a new hat," I said.

He smiled. I took his arm; slowly we set off along Vrede Street.

"Let me tell you the dream I had," I said. "The man in my dream didn't have a hat, but I think it was you. He had long oily hair brushed straight back from his forehead." Long and oily; dirty too, hanging down at the back in ugly rats' tails; but I did not mention that.

"We were at the seaside. He was teaching me to swim. He held me by the hands and drew me out while I lay flat and kicked. I was wearing a knitted costume, the kind we had in the old days, navy blue. I was a child. But then in dreams we are always children.

"He was drawing me out, backing into the sea, fixing me with his eyes. He had eyes like yours. There were no waves, just a ripple of water coming in, glinting with light. In fact the water was oily too. Where his body broke the surface the oil clung to him with the heavy sheen oil has. I thought to myself: sardine oil: I am the little sardine: he is taking me out into the oil. I wanted to say *Turn back,* but dared not open my mouth for fear the oil would flood in and fill my lungs. Drowning in oil: I had not the courage for that."

I paused to let him speak, but he was silent. We turned the corner into Schoonder Street.

"Of course I am not telling you this dream innocently," I said. "Retailing a dream is always meant to achieve something. The question is, what?

"The day I first saw you behind the garage was the day I had the bad news about myself, about my case. It was too much of a coincidence. I wondered whether you were not, if you will excuse the word, an angel come to show me the way. Of course you were not, are not, cannot be—I see that. But that is only half the story, isn't it? We half-perceive but we also half-create.

"So I have continued to tell myself stories in which you lead, I follow. And if you say not a word, that is, I tell myself, because the angel is wordless. The angel goes before, the woman follows. His eyes are open, he sees; hers are shut, she is still sunk in the sleep of worldliness. That is why I keep turning to you for guidance, for help."

The front door was locked but the gate to the courtyard swung open. The broken glass had not been swept up, the door to Florence's room hung askew. I cast my gaze down, treading carefully, not ready yet to look into the room, not strong enough.

The kitchen door was unlocked. They had not found the key.

"Come in," I said to Vercueil.

The house was and was not as it had been. Things in the kitchen were out of place. My umbrella hung where it had never hung before. The sofa had been shifted, exposing an old stain on the carpet. And over all a strange smell: not only cigarette smoke and sweat but something sharp and penetrating that I could not place. They have left their mark on everything, I thought: thorough workers. Then I remembered the file on my desk, the letter, all the pages thus far. That too! I thought: they will have been through that too! Soiled fingers turning the pages, eyes without love going over the naked words. "Help me upstairs," I said to Vercueil.

The file, left open when I last wrote, was closed. The lock of the filing cabinet was broken. There were gaps in the bookshelves.

The two unused rooms had had their locks forced.

They had been through the cupboard, the chest of drawers. Nothing left untouched. Like the last visit the burglars paid. The search a mere pretext. The true purpose the touching, the fingering. The spirit malevolent. Like rape: a way of filthying a woman.

I turned to Vercueil, wordless, sick to my stomach.

"There's someone downstairs," he said.

From the landing we could hear someone talking on the telephone.

The voice stopped. A young man in uniform emerged into the hallway and nodded to us.

"What are you doing in my house?" I called down.

"Just checking," he replied quite cheerfully. "We didn't want strangers coming in." He gathered up a cap, a coat, a rifle. Was it the rifle I had smelled? "The detectives will be here at eight," he said. "I'll wait outside." He smiled; he seemed to think he had done me a service; he seemed to be expecting thanks.

"I must have a bath," I said to Vercueil.

But I did not have a bath. I closed the bedroom door, took two of the red pills, and lay down trembling all over. The trembling got worse till I was shaking like a leaf in a storm. I was cold but the trembling was not from the cold.

A minute at a time, I told myself: do not fall to pieces now: think only of the next minute.

The trembling began to subside.

Man, I thought: the only creature with a part of his existence in the unknown, in the future, like a shadow cast before him. Trying continually to catch up with that moving shadow, to inhabit the image of his hope. But I, I cannot afford to be man. Must be something smaller, blinder, closer to the ground.

There was a knock and Vercueil came in, followed by the policeman who yesterday had worn the reindeer jersey and now wore a jacket and tie. The trembling began again. He motioned for Vercueil to leave the room. I sat up. "Don't go, Mr. Vercueil," I said; and to him: "What right have you to come into my house?"

"We have been worried about you." He did not seem worried at all. "Where were you last night?" And then, when I did not reply: "Are you sure you are all right by yourself, Mrs. Curren?"

Though I clenched my fists, the trembling grew worse till it convulsed me. "I am not by myself!" I screamed at him: "You are the one who is by himself!"

He was not taken aback. On the contrary, he seemed to be encouraging me to go on.

Hold yourself together! I thought. They will commit you, they will call you mad and take you away!

"What do you want here?" I asked more quietly.

"I just want to ask a few questions. How did you come across this boy Johannes?"

Johannes: was that his true name? Surely not.

"He was a friend of my domestic's son. A school friend."

Out of his pocket he brought a little cassette recorder and set it on the bed beside me.

"And where is your domestic's son?"

"He is dead and buried. Surely you know these things."

"What happened to him?"

"He was shot out on the Flats."

"And are there any more of them that you know of?"

"More of whom?"

"More friends."

"Thousands. Millions. More than you can count."

"I mean, more from that cell. Are there any others who have used your premises?"

"No."

"And do you know how these arms came into their hands?"

"What arms?"

"A pistol. Three detonators."

"I know nothing about detonators. I don't know what a detonator is. The pistol was mine."

"Did they take it from you?"

"I lent it to them. Not to them. To the boy, John."

"You lent him the pistol? Was the pistol yours?"

"Yes."

"Why did you lend him the pistol?"

"To defend himself."

"To defend himself against who, Mrs. Curren?"

"To defend himself against attack."

"And what kind of pistol was it, Mrs. Curren? Can you show me the license for it?"

"I know nothing about kinds of pistol. I have had it for a long time, from before all this fuss about licenses."

"Are you sure you gave it to him? You know this is a chargeable offense we are talking about."

The pills were beginning to take effect. The pain in my back grew more distant, my limbs relaxed, the horizon began to expand again.

"Do you really want to go on with this nonsense?" I said. I lay back on the pillow and closed my eyes. My head was spinning. "These are dead people we are talking about. There is nothing more you can do to them. They are safe. You have had the execution. Why bother with a trial? Why not just close the case?"

He picked up the recorder, fiddled with it, put it back on the pillow. "Just checking," he said.

With a languorous arm I brushed the recorder away. He caught it before it hit the floor.

"You have been through my private papers," I said. "You have taken books that belong to me. I want them back. I want everything back. All my things. They are no business of yours."

"We are not going to eat your books, Mrs. Curren. You will get everything back in the end."

"I don't want things back in the end. I want them back now. They are mine. They are private."

He shook his head. "This is not private, Mrs. Curren. You know that. Nothing is private anymore."

The languor was getting to my tongue now. "Leave me," I said thickly.

"Just a few more questions. Where were you last night?"

"With Mr. Vercueil."

"Is this Mr. Vercueil?"

It took too much of an effort to open my eyes. "Yes," I murmured.

"Who is Mr. Vercueil?" And then, in quite a different tone: *"Wie is jy?"*

"Mr. Vercueil takes care of me. Mr. Vercueil is my right-hand man. Come here, Mr. Vercueil."

I reached out and found Vercueil's trouser leg, then his hand, the bad hand with the curled fingers. With the numb, clawlike grip of the old I clung to it.

"In Godsnaam," said the detective somewhere far away. In God's name: mere fulmination, or a curse on the pair of us? My grip broke, I began to slide away.

A word appeared before me: Thabanchu, Thaba Nchu. I tried to concentrate. Nine letters, anagram for what? With a great effort I placed the *b* first. Then I was gone.

I awoke thirsty, groggy, full of pain. The clockface stared at me but I could make no sense of the hands. The house was silent with the silence of deserted houses.

Thabanchu: *banch? bath?* With stupid hands I unwrapped the sheet from around me. Must I have a bath?

But my feet did not take me to the bathroom. Holding on

to the rail, bent over, groaning, I went downstairs and dialed the Guguletu number. On and on the phone rang. Then at last someone answered, a child, a girl. "Is Mr. Thabane there?" I asked. "No." "Then can I speak to Mrs. Mkubuleki—no, not Mrs. Mkubuleki, Mrs. Mkubukeli?" "Mrs. Mkubukeli does not live here." "But do you know Mrs. Mkubukeli?" "Yes, I know him." "Mrs. Mkubukeli?" "Yes." "Who are you?" "I am Lily." Lee-lee. "Are you the only one at home?" "There is my sister too." "How old is your sister?" "She is six." "And you—how old are you?" "Ten." "Can you take a message to Mrs. Mkubukeli, Lily?" "Yes." "It is about her brother Mr. Thabane. She must tell Mr. Thabane to be careful. Say it is very important. Mr. Thabane must be careful. My name is Mrs. Curren. Can you write that down? And this is my number." I read out the number, spelled my name. Mrs. Curren: nine letters, anagram for what?

Vercueil knocked and came in. "Do you want something to eat?" he said.

"I am not hungry. But help yourself to anything you can find."

I wanted to be left alone. But he lingered, eyeing me curiously. I was sitting up in bed, gloves on my hands, the writing pad on my knees. For half an hour I had sat with the page blank before me.

"I am just waiting for my hands to warm up," I said.

But it was not cold fingers that kept me from writing. It was the pills, which I take more of now, and more often. They are like smoke flares. I swallow them and they release a fog inside me, a fog of extinction. I cannot take the pills and go on with the writing. So without pain no writing: a new and terrible rule. Except that, when I have taken the pills, nothing is terrible anymore, everything is indifferent, everything is the same.

Nevertheless I do write. In the dead of night, with Vercueil asleep downstairs, I take up this letter to tell you one more thing about that "John," that sullen boy I never took to. I want to tell you that, despite my dislike of him, he is with me more clearly, more piercingly than Bheki has ever been. He is with me or I am with him: him or the trace of him. It is the middle of the night but it is the gray of his last morning too. I am here in my bed but I am there in Florence's room too, with its one window and one door and no other way out. Outside the door men are waiting, crouched like hunters, to present the boy with his death. In his lap he holds the pistol that, for this interval, keeps the hunters at bay, that was his and Bheki's great secret, that was going to make men of them; and beside him I stand or hover. The barrel of the pistol is between his knees; he strokes it up and down. He is listening to the murmur of voices outside, and I listen with him. He is readying himself for the smoke that will choke his lungs, the kick that will burst the door open, the torrent of fire that will sweep him away. He is readying himself to raise the pistol in that instant and fire the one shot he will have time to fire into the heart of the light.

His eyes are unblinking, fixed on the door through which he is going to leave the world. His mouth is dry but he is not afraid. His heart beats steadily like a fist in his chest clenching and unclenching.

His eyes are open and mine, though I write, are shut. My eyes are shut in order to see.

Within this interval there is no time, though his heart beats time. I am here in my room in the night but I am also with him, all the time, as I am with you across the seas, hovering.

A hovering time, but not eternity. A *time being,* a suspension, before the return of the time in which the door bursts open and we face, first he, then I, the great white glare.

four

I have had a dream of Florence, a dream or vision. In the dream I see her striding again down Government Avenue holding Hope by the hand and carrying Beauty on her back. All three of them wear masks. I am there too, with a crowd of people of all kinds and conditions gathered around me. The air is festive. I am to provide a show.

But Florence does not stop to watch. Gaze fixed ahead, she passes as if through a congregation of wraiths.

The eyes of her mask are like eyes in pictures from the

ancient Mediterranean: large, oval, with the pupil in the center: the almond eyes of a goddess.

I stand in the middle of the Avenue opposite the Parliament buildings, circled by people, doing my tricks with fire. Over me tower great oaks. But my mind is not on my tricks. I am intent on Florence. Her dark coat, her dull dress have fallen away. In a white slip ruffled by the wind, her feet bare, her head bare, her right breast bare, she strides past, the one child, masked, naked, trotting quickly beside her, the other stretching an arm out over her shoulder, pointing.

Who is this goddess who comes in a vision with uncovered breast cutting the air? It is Aphrodite, but not smile-loving Aphrodite, patroness of pleasures: an older figure, a figure of urgency, of cries in the dark, short and sharp, of blood and earth, emerging for an instant, showing herself, passing.

From the goddess comes no call, no signal. Her eye is open and is blank. She sees and does not see.

Burning, doing my show, I stand transfixed. The flames flowing from me are blue as ice. I feel no pain.

It is a vision from last night's dream time but also from outside time. Forever the goddess is passing, forever, caught in a posture of surprise and regret, I do not follow. Though I peer and peer into the vortex from which visions come, the wake of the goddess and her god-children remains empty, the woman who should follow behind not there, the woman with serpents of flame in her hair who beats her arms and cries and dances.

I related the dream to Vercueil.

"Is it real?" he asked.

"Real? Of course not. It isn't even authentic. Florence has

nothing to do with Greece. Figures in dreams have another kind of import. They are signs, signs of other things."

"Were they real? Was she real?" he repeated, bringing me up short, refusing to be deflected. "What else did you see?"

"What else? Is there more? Do you know?" I said more softly, feeling my way after him now.

He shook his head, baffled.

"All the days you have known me," I said, "I have been standing on the riverbank awaiting my turn. I am waiting for someone to show me the way across. Every minute of every day I am here, waiting. That is what else I see. Do you see it too?"

He said nothing.

"The reason I fight against going back to hospital is that in hospital they will put me to sleep. That is the expression they use for animals, as a kindness, but they may as well use it for people. They will put me into a sleep without dreams. They will feed me mandragora till I grow drowsy and fall into the river and am drowned and washed away. That way I will never cross. I cannot allow it to happen. I have come too far. I cannot have my eyes closed."

"What do you want to see?" said Vercueil.

"I want to see you as you really are."

Diffidently he shrugged. "Who am I?"

"Just a man. A man who came without being invited. More I can't say yet. Can you?"

He shook his head. "No."

"If you want to do something for me," I said, "you can fix the aerial for the radio."

"Don't you want me to bring the television up instead?"

"I haven't the stomach to watch television. It will make me sick."

"Television can't make you sick. It's just pictures."

"There is no such thing as just pictures. There are men behind the pictures. They send out their pictures to make people sick. You know what I am talking about."

"Pictures can't make you sick."

Sometimes he does this: contradicts me, provokes me, chips away at me, watching for signs of irritation. It is his way of teasing, so clumsy, so unappealing that my heart quite goes out to him.

"Fix the aerial, please, that's all I ask."

He went downstairs. Minutes later he came stamping up with the television set in his arms. He plugged it in facing the bed, switched it on, fiddled with the aerial, stood aside. It was midafternoon. Against blue sky a flag waved. A brass band played the anthem of the Republic.

"Switch it off," I said.

He turned the sound louder.

"Switch it off!" I screamed.

He wheeled, took in my angry glare. Then, to my surprise, he began to do a little shuffle. Swaying his hips, holding his hands out, clicking his fingers, he danced, unmistakably danced, to music I never thought could be danced to. He was mouthing words too. What were they? Not, certainly, the words I knew.

"Off!" I screamed again.

An old woman, toothless, in a rage: I must have looked a sight. He turned the sound down.

"Off!"

He switched it off. "Don't get so upset," he murmured.

"Then don't be silly, Vercueil. And don't make fun of me. Don't trivialize me."

"Still, why get in a state?"

"Because I am afraid of going to hell and having to listen to *Die stem* for all eternity."

He shook his head. "Don't worry," he said, "it's all going to end. Have patience."

"I haven't got time for patience. You may have time but I haven't got time."

Again he shook his head. "Maybe you've also got time," he whispered, and gave me his toothed leer.

For an instant it was as if the heavens opened and light blazed down. Hungry for good news after a lifetime of bad news, unable to help myself, I smiled back. "Really?" I said. He nodded. Like two fools we grinned each at the other. He clicked his fingers suggestively; awkward as a gannet, all feathers and bone, he repeated a step of his dance. Then he went out, climbed the ladder, and joined the broken wire, and I had the radio again.

But what was there to listen to? The airwaves so bulge nowadays with the nations peddling their wares that music is all but squeezed out. I fell asleep to *An American in Paris* and awoke to a steady patter of morse. Where did it come from? From a ship at sea? From some old-fashioned steamship plying the waves between Walvis Bay and Ascension Island? The dots and dashes followed on without haste, without falter, in a stream that promised to flow till the cows came home. What was their message? Did it matter? Their patter, like rain, a rain of meaning, comforted me, made the night bearable as I lay waiting for the hour to roll round for the next pill.

•

I say I do not want to be put to sleep. The truth is, without sleep I cannot endure. Whatever else it brings, the Diconal at least brings sleep or a simulacrum of sleep. As the pain recedes, as time quickens, as the horizon lifts, my attention, concentrated like a burning glass on the pain, can slacken for a while; I can draw breath, unclench my balled hands, straighten my legs. Give thanks for this mercy, I say to myself: for the sick body stunned, for the soul drowsy, half out of its casing, beginning to float.

But the respite is never long. Clouds come over, thoughts begin to bunch, to take on the dense, angry life of a swarm of flies. I shake my head, trying to clear them away. This is my hand, I say, opening my eyes wide, staring at the veins on the back of my hand; this is the bedspread. Then as quick as lightning something strikes. In an instant I am gone and in another instant I am back, still staring at my hand. Between these instants an hour may have passed or the blink of an eye, during which I have been absent, gone, struggling with something thick and rubbery that invades the mouth and grips the tongue at its root, something that comes from the depths of the sea. I surface, shaking my head like a swimmer. In my throat is a taste of bile, of sulfur. Madness! I say to myself: this is what it tastes like to be mad!

Once I came to myself facing the wall. In my hand was a pencil, its point broken. All over the wall were sprawling, sliding characters, meaningless, coming from me or someone inside me.

I telephoned Dr. Syfret. "My reaction to the Diconal seems

to be getting worse," I said, and tried to describe it. "I wonder, is there no alternative you can prescribe?"

"I was not aware that you still regarded yourself as under my care," replied Dr. Syfret. "You should be in hospital getting proper attention. I can't conduct a surgery over the telephone."

"I am asking for very little," I said. "The Diconal is giving me hallucinations. Is there nothing else I can take?"

"And I say, I can't treat you without seeing you. That is not how I work, that is not how any of my colleagues work."

I was silent so long he must have thought he had lost me. The truth was, I was wavering. Don't you understand? I wanted to say: I am tired, tired unto death. *In manus tuas:* take me into your hands, care for me, or, if you cannot, do whatever is next best.

"Let me ask one last question," I said. "The reactions I am having—do other people have them too?"

"Patients react in many different ways. Yes, it is possible your reactions are due to the Diconal."

"Then if by some chance you have a change of heart," I said, "could you telephone a new prescription through to the Avalon Pharmacy in Mill Street? I have no illusions about my condition, doctor. It is not care I need, just help with the pain."

"And if you change your mind and want to see me at any time, Mrs. Curren, day or night, you have only to pick up the telephone."

An hour later the doorbell rang. It was the deliveryman from the pharmacy bringing a new prescription in a fourteen-day supply.

I telephoned the pharmacist. "Tylox," I asked, "is that the strongest?"

"What do you mean?"

"I mean, is it the last one prescribed?"

"That is not the way it works, Mrs. Curren. There is no first and no last."

I took two of the new pills. Again the miraculous draining away of pain, the euphoria, the feeling of being restored to life. I had a bath, got back into bed, tried to read, fell into a confused sleep. In an hour I was awake again. The pain was creeping back, bringing with it nausea and the first edge of the familiar shadow of depression.

The drug over the pain: a shaft of light but then darkness redoubled.

Vercueil came in.

"I have taken the new pills," I said. "They are no improvement. Slightly stronger, perhaps; that's all."

"Take more," said Vercueil. "You don't have to wait four hours."

A drunkard's advice.

"I'm sure I will," I said. "But if I am free to take them whenever I like, why not take them all together?"

There was silence between us.

"Why did you choose me?" I said.

"I didn't choose you."

"Why did you come here, to this house?"

"You didn't have a dog."

"Why else?"

"I thought you wouldn't make trouble."

"And have I made trouble?"

He came toward me. His face was puffy, I could smell liquor on his breath. "If you want me to help you I'll help you," he said. He leaned over and took me by the throat, his thumbs resting lightly on my larynx, the three bad fingers bunched under my ear. "Don't," I whispered, and pushed his hands away. My eyes swam with tears. I took his hands in mine and beat them on my chest in a gesture of lamentation quite foreign to me.

After a while I was still. He continued to lean over me, allowing me to use him. The dog put its nose over the edge of the bed, sniffing at us.

"Will you let the dog sleep with me?" I said.

"Why?"

"For the warmth."

"He won't stay. He sleeps where I sleep."

"Then sleep here too."

There was a long wait while he went downstairs. I had another pill. Then the light on the landing went off. I heard him take off his shoes. "Take off the hat too, for a change," I said.

He lay down at my back, on top of the bedclothes. The smell of his dirty feet reached me. He whistled softly; the dog leapt up, did its circle dance, settled between his legs and mine. Like Tristan's sword, keeping us honest.

The pill worked its wonders. For half an hour, while he and the dog slept, I lay still, free of pain, my soul alert, darting. A vision passed before my eyes of the child Beauty riding toward me on her mother's back, bobbing, staring imperiously ahead. Then the vision faded and clouds of dust, the dust of Borodino, came rolling over my sight like the wheels of the carriage of death.

I switched on the lamp. It was midnight.

I will draw a veil soon. This was never meant to be the story of a body, but of the soul it houses. I will not show to you what you will not be able to bear: a woman in a burning house running from window to window, calling through the bars for help.

Vercueil and his dog, sleeping so calmly beside these torrents of grief. Fulfilling their charge, waiting for the soul to emerge. The soul, neophyte, wet, blind, ignorant.

I have the story now of how he lost the use of his fingers. It was in an accident at sea. They had to abandon ship. In the scramble his hand was caught in a pulley and crushed. All night he floated on a raft with seven other men and a boy, in agony. The next day they were picked up by a Russian trawler and his hand was given attention. But by then it was too late.

"Did you learn any Russian?" I asked.

All he remembered, he said, was *xorosho*.

"No one mentioned Borodino?"

"I don't remember Borodino."

"You didn't think of staying with the Russians?"

He looked at me strangely.

He has never been to sea since then.

"Don't you miss the sea?" I asked.

"I'll never set foot in a boat again," he replied decidedly.

"Why?"

"Because next time I won't be so lucky."

"How do you know? If you had faith in yourself you could walk on water. Don't you believe in the doings of faith?"

He was silent.

"Or a whirlwind would arrive and pluck you out of the water and set you down on dry land. And there are always dolphins. Dolphins rescue drowning sailors, don't they? Why did you become a sailor anyway?"

"You don't always think ahead. You don't always know."

I pinched his ring finger lightly. "Can't you feel anything?"

"No. The nerves are dead."

I always knew he had a story to tell, and now he begins to tell it, starting with the fingers of one hand. A mariner's story. Do I believe it? Verily, I do not care. There is no lie that does not have at its core some truth. One must only know how to listen.

He has worked at the docks too, lifting things, loading things. One day, he said, unloading a crate, they smelled something bad and opened it and found the body of a man, a stowaway who had starved to death in his hiding place.

"Where did he come from?" I asked.

"China. A long way away."

He has also worked for the SPCA, at their kennels.

"Was that where you got to like dogs?"

"I always got on with dogs."

"Did you have a dog as a child?"

"Mm," he said, meaning nothing. Early on he decided he could get away with choosing which of my questions to hear, which not to hear.

Nevertheless, piece by piece I put together the story of a life as obscure as any on earth. What is in store for him next, I wonder, when the episode of the old woman in the big house is over with? One hand crippled, unable to do all its offices. His sailor's skill with knots lost. Not dextrous anymore, nor fully decent. In the middle years of his course, and at his side no wife. Alone: *stoksielalleen:* a stick in an empty field, a soul alone, sole. Who will watch over him?

"What will you do with yourself when I am gone?"

"I will go on."

"I am sure you will; but who will there be in your life?"

Cautiously he smiled. "Do I need somebody in my life?"

Not a riposte. A real question. He does not know. He is asking me, this rudimentary man.

"Yes. I would say you need a wife, if the idea does not strike you as eccentric. Even that woman you brought here, as long as there is feeling for her in your heart."

He shook his head.

"Never mind. It is not marriage I am talking about but something else. I would promise to watch over you, except that I have no firm idea of what is possible after death. Perhaps there will be no watching over allowed, or very little. All these places have their rules, and, whatever one may wish, it may not be possible to get around them. There may not even be secrets allowed, secret watching. There may be no way of keeping a space in the heart private for you or anyone else. All may be erased. All. It is a terrible thought. Enough to make one rebel, to make one say: If that is how things are to be, I withdraw: here is my ticket, I am handing it back. But I doubt very much that the handing back of tickets will be allowed, for whatever reason.

"That is why you should not be so alone. Because I may have to go away entirely."

He sat on the bed with his back to me, bent over, gripping the dog's head between his knees, stroking it.

"Do you understand me?"

"Mm." The *mm* that could mean yes but in fact means nothing.

"No, you don't. You don't understand at all. It is not the

prospect of your solitude that appalls me. It is the prospect of my own."

Every day he goes off to do the shopping. In the evenings he cooks, then hovers over me, watching to see that I eat. I am never hungry but haven't the heart to tell him. "I find it hard to eat while you watch," I say as gently as I can, then hide the food and feed it to the dog.

His favorite concoction is white bread fried in egg with tuna on the bread and tomato sauce on the tuna. I wish I had had the foresight to give him cooking lessons.

Though he has the whole house to spread himself in, he lives, in effect, with me in my room. He drops empty packets, old wrapping papers on the floor. When there is a draft they scud around like ghosts. "Take the rubbish away," I plead. "I will," he promises, and sometimes does, but then leaves more.

We share a bed, folded one upon the other like a page folded in two, like two wings folded: old mates, bunkmates, conjoined, conjugal. *Lectus genialis, lectus adversus.* His toenails, when he takes off his shoes, are yellow, almost brown, like horn. Feet that he keeps out of water for fear of falling: falling into depths where he cannot breathe. A dry creature, a creature of air, like those locust fairies in Shakespeare with their whipstock of cricket's bone, lash of spider film. Huge swarms of them borne out to sea on the wind, out of sight of land, tiring, settling one upon another upon another, resolving to drown the Atlantic by their numbers. Swallowed, all of them, to the last. Brittle wings on the sea floor sighing like a forest of leaves; dead eyes by the million; and the crabs moving among them, clutching, grinding.

He snores.

From the side of her shadow husband your mother writes.

Forgive me if the picture offends you. One must love what is nearest. One must love what is to hand, as a dog loves.

Mrs. V.

September 23, the equinox. Steady rain falling from a sky that has closed in tight against the mountain, so low that one could reach up with a broomstick and touch it. A soothing, muffling sound, like a great hand, a hand of water, folding over the house; the patter on the roof tiles, the ripple in the gutters ceasing to be noise, become a thickening, a liquefaction of the air.

"What is this?" asked Vercueil.

He had a little hinged rosewood case. Held open at a certain angle to the light, it reveals a young man with long hair in an old-fashioned suit. Change the angle, and the image decomposes into silver streaks behind a glass surface.

"It is a photograph from the olden days. From before photographs."

"Who is it?"

"I am not sure. It may be one of my grandfather's brothers."

"Your house is like a museum."

(He has been poking around in the rooms the police broke into.)

"In a museum things have labels. This is a museum where the labels have fallen off. A museum in decay. A museum that ought to be in a museum."

"You should sell these old things if you don't want them."

"Sell them if you like. Sell me too."

"For what?"

"For bones. For hair. Sell my teeth too. Unless you think

I am worth nothing. It's a pity we don't have one of those carts that children used to wheel the Guy around in. You could wheel me down the Avenue with a letter pinned to my front. Then you could set fire to me. Or you could take me to some more obscure place, the rubbish dump for instance, and dispose of me there."

He used to go out onto the balcony when he wanted to smoke. Now he smokes on the landing and the smoke drifts back into my room. I cannot stand it. But it is time to begin getting used to what I cannot stand.

He came upon me washing my underwear in the basin. I was in pain from the bending: no doubt I looked terrible. "I will do that for you," he offered. I refused. But then I could not reach the line, so he had to hang it for me: an old woman's underwear, gray, listless.

When the pain bites deepest and I shudder and go pale and a cold sweat breaks out on me, he sometimes holds my hand. I twist in his grip like a hooked fish; I am aware of an ugly look on my face, the look people have when they are rapt in lovemaking: brutal, predatory. He does not like that look; he turns his eyes away. As for me, I think: let him see, let him learn what it is like!

He carries a knife in his pocket. Not a clasp knife but a menacing blade with a sharp point embedded in a cork. When he gets into bed he puts it on the floor beside him, with his money.

So I am well guarded. Death would think twice before trying to pass this dog, this man.

What is Latin? he asked.

A dead language, I replied, a language spoken by the dead.

"Really?" he said. The idea seemed to tickle him.

"Yes, really," I said. "You only hear it at funerals nowadays. Funerals and the odd wedding."

"Can you speak it?"

I recited some Virgil, Virgil on the unquiet dead:

> nec ripas datur horrendas et rauca fluenta
> transportare prius quam sedibus ossa quierunt.
> centum errant annos volitantque haec litora circum;
> tum demum admissi stagna exoptata revisunt.

"What does it mean?" he said.

"It means that if you don't mail the letter to my daughter I will have a hundred years of misery."

"It doesn't."

"Yes, it does. *Ossa:* that is the word for a diary. Something on which the days of your life are inscribed."

Later he came back. "Say the Latin again," he asked. I spoke the lines and watched his lips move as he listened. He is memorizing, I thought. But it was not so. It was the dactyl beating in him, with its power to move the pulse, the throat.

"Was that what you taught? Was that your job?"

"Yes, it was my job. I made a living from it. Giving voice to the dead."

"And who paid you?"

"The taxpayers. The people of South Africa, both great and small."

"Could you teach me?"

"I could have taught you. I could have taught you most things Roman. I am not so sure about the Greek. I could still teach you, but there would not be time for everything."

He was flattered, I could see.

"You would find Latin easy," I said. "There would be much you remembered."

Another challenge issued, another intimation that *I know.* I am like a woman with a husband who keeps a mistress on the sly, scolding him, coaxing him to come clean. But my hints pass him by. He is not hiding anything. His ignorance is real. His ignorance, his innocence.

"There is something that won't come, isn't there?" I said. "Why don't you just speak and see where the words take you?"

But he was at a threshold he could not cross. He stood, balked, wordless, hiding behind the cigarette smoke, narrowing his eyes so that I should not see in.

The dog circled him, came to me, drifted off again, restless.

Is it possible that the dog is the one sent, and not he?

You will never get to see him, I suppose. I would have liked to send you a picture, but my camera was taken in the last burglary. In any case, he is not the kind of person who photographs well. I have seen the picture on his identity card. He looks like a prisoner torn from the darkness of a cell, thrust into a room full of blinding lights, shoved against a wall, shouted at to stand still. His image raped from him, taken by force. He is like one of those half-mythical creatures that come out in photographs only as blurs, vague forms disappearing into the undergrowth that could be man or beast or merely a bad spot on the emulsion: unproved, unattested. Or disappearing over the edge of the picture, leaving behind in the shutter trap an arm or a leg or the back of a head.

"Would you like to go to America?" I asked him.

"Why?"

"To take my letter. Instead of mailing it, you could take

it in person: fly to America and fly back. It would be an adventure. Better than sailing. My daughter would meet you and take care of you. I would buy the ticket in advance. Would you go?"

He smiled bravely. But some of my jokes touch a sore spot, I know.

"I am serious," I said.

But the truth is, it is not a serious suggestion. Vercueil with a haircut, in shop clothes, mooning about in your guest bedroom, desperate for a drink, too shy to ask; and you in the next room, the children asleep, your husband asleep, poring over this letter, this confession, this madness—it does not bear thinking of. *I do not need this,* you say to yourself through gritted teeth. *This is what I came here to get away from, why does it have to follow me?*

With time on my hands, I have been shuffling through the pictures you have sent from America over the years, looking at the backgrounds, at all the things that fell willy-nilly within the frame at the instant you pressed the button. In the picture you sent of the two boys in their canoe, for instance, my eye wanders from their faces to the ripples on the lake and the deep green of the fir trees and then back to the orange life jackets they wear, like water wings of old. The dull, bland sheen of their surfaces quite hypnotizes me. Rubber or plastic or something in between: some substance coarse to the touch, tough. Why is it that this material, foreign to me, foreign perhaps to humankind, shaped, sealed, inflated, tied to the bodies of your children, signifies so intensely for me the world you now live in, and why does it make my spirit sink? I have no idea. But since this writing has time and again taken me from where I have no idea to where I begin to have an idea, let me say, in all tentativeness, that perhaps it dispirits me that your children will never drown. All those lakes, all that water: a land of lakes and rivers: yet if by some mischance they ever tip out of their canoe, they will bob safely in the water, supported by their bright orange wings, till a motorboat comes to pick them up and bear them off and all is well again.

A recreation area, you call it on the back of the photograph. The lake tamed, the forest tamed, renamed.

You say you will have no more children. The line runs out, then, in these two boys, seed planted in the American snows, who will never drown, whose life expectancy is seventy-five and rising. Even I, who live on shores where the waters swallow grown men, where life expectancy declines every year, am having a death without illumination. What can these two poor underprivileged boys paddling about in their recreation area hope for? They will die at seventy-five or eighty-five as stupid as when they were born.

Do I wish death upon my grandchildren? Are you, at this very instant, flinging the page away from you in disgust? *Mad old woman!* are you crying out?

They are not my grandchildren. They are too distant to be children of mine of whatever sort. I do not leave behind a numerous family. A daughter. A consort and his dog.

By no means do I wish death upon them. The two boys whose lives have brushed mine are in any event already dead. No, I wish your children life. But the wings you have tied on them will not guarantee them life. Life is dust between the toes. Life is dust between the teeth. Life is biting the dust.

Or: life is drowning. Falling through water, to the floor.

•

The time is nearly upon me when I will have to depend on help for the most intimate things. High time, then, to put an end to this sorry story. Not that I doubt Vercueil would help. When it comes to last things, I no longer doubt him in any way. There has always been in him a certain hovering if undependable solicitude for me, a solicitude he knows no way of expressing. I have fallen and he has caught me. It is not he who fell under my care when he arrived, I now understand, nor I who fell under his: we fell under each other, and have tumbled and risen since then in the flights and swoops of that mutual election.

Yet he is as far from being a nurse, a *nourrice,* a nourisher, as I can imagine. He is dry. His drink is not water but fire. Perhaps that is why I cannot imagine children of his: because his semen would be dry, dry and brown, like pollen or like the dust of this country.

I need his presence, his comfort, his help, but he needs help too. He needs the help only a woman can give a man. Not a seduction but an induction. He does not know how to love. I speak not of the motions of the soul but of something simpler. He does not know how to love as a boy does not know how to love. Does not know what zips and buttons and clasps to expect. Does not know what goes where. Does not know how to do what he has to do.

The nearer end comes, the more faithful he is. Yet still I have to guide his hand.

I remember the day when we sat in the car, when he held out the matches to me and told me to *Do it.* I was outraged. But was I fair to him? It seems to me now that he has no more conception of death than a virgin has of sex. But the same curiosity. The curiosity of a dog that sniffs at one's crotch, wagging its tail, its tongue hanging out red and stupid as a penis.

Yesterday, as he was helping me into the bath, my robe slipped open and I caught him staring. Like those children on Mill Street: no decency in him. Decency: the inexplicable: the ground of all ethics. Things we do not do. We do not stare when the soul leaves the body, but veil our eyes with tears or cover them with our hands. We do not stare at scars, which are places where the soul has struggled to leave and been forced back, closed up, sewn in.

I asked him whether he was still feeding the cats. "Yes," he said, lying. For the cats are gone, chased out. Do I care? No, not anymore. After I have cared for you, for him, there is little space left in my heart. The rest must, as they say, go to pot.

Last night, growing terribly cold, I tried to call you up to say good-bye. But you would not come. I whispered your name. "My daughter, my child," I whispered into the darkness; but all that appeared to me was a photograph: a picture of you, not you. Severed, I thought: that line severed too. Now there is nothing to hold me.

But I fell asleep, and woke up, and was still here, and this morning feel quite strong. So perhaps it is not only I who do the calling. Perhaps when I grow cold it is because I am being called out of my body across the seas, and do not know it.

As you see, I still believe in your love.

I am going to release you soon from this rope of words. There is no need to be sorry for me. But spare a thought for this man left behind who cannot swim, does not yet know how to fly.

•

I slept and woke up cold: my belly, my heart, my very bones cold. The door to the balcony was open, the curtains were waving in the wind.

Vercueil stood on the balcony staring out over a sea of rustling leaves. I touched his arm, his high, peaked shoulders, the bony ridge of his spine. Through chattering teeth I spoke: "What are you looking at?"

He did not answer. I stood closer. A sea of shadows beneath us, and the screen of leaves shifting, rustling, like scales over the darkness.

"Is it time?" I said.

I got back into bed, into the tunnel between the cold sheets. The curtains parted; he came in beside me. For the first time I smelled nothing. He took me in his arms and held me with mighty force, so that the breath went out of me in a rush. From that embrace there was no warmth to be had.

1986–89

LONDON FIELDS
by Martin Amis

Two murders in the making: the first, of a femme fatale intent on goading one of her lovers into killing her, and the other, that of the Earth itself.

"An uninhibited high-energy performance...[Amis] is one of the most gifted novelists of his generation."

—*Time*

0-679-73034-6/$11.00

. . . .

A HISTORY OF THE WORLD IN 10½ CHAPTERS
by Julian Barnes

A hilariously revisionist account of the voyage of Noah's ark—with a sneak preview of heaven—that is "by turns funny, harrowing, satirical, consolatory, absurd" *(Washington Post Book World)*.

0-679-73137-7/$9.95

. . . .

THE SHELTERING SKY
by Paul Bowles

The story of three American travelers adrift in the cities and deserts of North Africa after the Second World War.

"His art far exceeds that of...the great American writers of our day."

—Gore Vidal

0-679-72979-8/$9.95

. . . .

THE STRANGER
by Albert Camus

Through the story of an ordinary man who unwittingly gets drawn into a senseless murder, Camus explores what he termed "the nakedness of man faced with the absurd."

0-679-72020-0/$7.95

. . . .

THE REMAINS OF THE DAY
by Kazuo Ishiguro

A profoundly compelling portrait of the perfect English butler and of his fading, insular world in postwar England.

"One of the best books of the year."

—*The New York Times Book Review*

0-679-73172-5/$9.95

. . . .

THE WOMAN WARRIOR
by Maxine Hong Kingston

"A remarkable book...As an account of growing up female and Chinese-American in California, in a laundry of course, it is anti-nostalgic; it burns the fat right out of the mind. As a dream—of the 'female avenger'—it is dizzying, elemental, a poem turned into a sword."

—*The New York Times*

0-679-72188-6/$9.00

. . . .

LOLITA
by Vladimir Nabokov

The controversial novel that tells the story of the aging Humbert Humbert's obsessive, devouring, and doomed passion for the nymphet Dolores Haze.

"The only convincing love story of our century."

—*Vanity Fair*

0-679-72316-1/$8.95

. . . .

THE PASSION
by Jeanette Winterson

Intertwining the destinies of two remarkable people—the soldier Henri, for eight years Napoleon's faithful cook, and Villanelle, the red-haired daughter of a Venetian boatman—*The Passion* is "a deeply imagined and beautiful book, often arrestingly so" *(The New York Times Book Review)*.

0-679-72437-0/$9.00

. . . .